HONESTY POLICY

Book 5 of the Thunderstrike Diaries

WENDY METCALFE

CHAPTER ONE

I'm a Predatorbot, and fierce female lions shouldn't spend their time worrying about humans. But we'd just left three of the Vatan sisters here on Davion, and I hoped that didn't turn out to be a huge mistake.

Bahar and I joined the troops in the shuttle. We launched at mid-morning, into a sky of thick grey cloud. It was going to rain down on Davion soon, and I was glad I'd avoided that. I don't enjoy getting wet. Well, what do you expect? I am a cat.

"Rain's starting," Bahar said as we lifted towards the clouds. "Should put out any bits of fire the tenders missed."

She was referring to the battle we'd recently been in down in the forest. Jorrak's rogue troops had been searching for the bunker we were holed up in. On reflection, my decision to go out and act as a diversion wasn't one of my finest.

"Jorrak's troops have all left, haven't they?" I asked.

"Relax, Snap." Strike's voice, relayed through the shuttle's nodes, held his usual exasperation at my fretting. "What's left of them have. We're the only Starnavy around here now. And we're going too."

Strike was a sneaky, smart, sapient machine intelligence, but he was so much more than that. He was the mind who ran the shipbody *Thunderstrike*, and he was my best friend in all the universe.

"Are we going Centralwards?" Bahar asked.

"Yes, captain, we are." That 'captain' definitely had a 'lower case letter', as Strike called it. Bahar didn't get to order Strike around, whatever her Starnavy rank.

The shuttle rose above the clouds into black sky, and I saw the bright shape of *Thunderstrike* above us. Davion's star threw highlights onto the curves of the ship's hull. *Thunderstrike* was all curves, and I thought he was beautiful.

We approached the big vehicle bay on the lowest deck, and Strike opened the airlock door as the shuttle came close. "Bringing you in now," he said. "Makes a change not having you shot at."

"Sure does," Bahar agreed.

I wondered how long that calm would last. We were less than a Standard away from Presidential elections, and current Collective President Jorrak was fighting for his reputation. We'd played a large part in uncovering his corruption and dodgy dealings.

Officially, Strike was like every other Starnavy frigate. Unofficially, he led the Special Investigations Unit. It was a huge network of contacts he'd built to ensure our elected officials kept on 'the straight and narrow', as he called it. Technically, we were traitors, but we tried not to spend much time thinking about that.

Strike landed the shuttle feather-light on its pad, and we waited while he repressurised the bay. I always found this waiting time tedious, but when I first came aboard *Thunderstrike* Strike had given me his 'Dangers of Space' presentation, so I knew I'd die if I walked out into vacuum. It wasn't a problem your ordinary planet-bound lion ever faced.

I tried to be patient as I waited for the bay to air up. Eventually Strike let us into his shipbody. Bahar and I rode up in the lift to Deck Two and went to the control room. I settled onto my belly in my space beside her captain's seat.

"I've been busy while you were away," Strike said. "I've been researching that outfit Merrill told us about, Sister Strategy. They're uncovering some worrying stuff."

"Like what?" Bahar asked.

"Like the rolling-back of rights for women across parts of the Collective. Six Central Worlds have made the sterilisation of women illegal. Penalties for domestic abusers are getting scaled back by judges sympathetic to Jorrak."

Bahar swore. "We have got to get that man removed from office."

"His influence has more subtle tendrils too," Strike continued. "Like withdrawal of funding to institutions with major women's education programmes."

"Here we go again," Bahar snarled. "I'm so tired of having to fight for my rights."

"I know. We'll get involved where we can, but I'm telling you this as backdrop, to explain the increasing tension in the Central Worlds. Sister Strategy seem to be operating out of Iku and Xan." Those were two planets quite close to Central Station and Earth. "They're good choices, as the Administration has minimal presences on both planets, surprisingly."

"So how do we find Nyla?" I asked.

"By starting with what we know about her. She's an

animal neuroscientist, so she's likely working on a research project somewhere. Problem is, I haven't found many likely candidates. Our President might have a hand in restricting funding for wildlife research too."

"Can't have humans finding out some animal's as smart as them," I said.

Bahar reached down and stroked my neck. "Several are," she said. "And you."

"Anyway," Strike continued, "I can't find any definitive record of Nyla on any project. I've done facial recognition scans of a hundred sets of project personnel. None of them look anything like her.

"There's another possibility. She's very good at political lobbying, and with the election coming up she might be doing that somewhere."

"Which is why you researched Sister Strategy?" Bahar asked.

"It's just a gut feel, but I suspect she's helping some outfit campaign against this President." Strike doesn't have a gut. But he does have the same instinctive feel for things that humans do.

"Why do you think she'd go politicking?" Bahar asked.

"Because Fia said Nyla has faced sexual discrimination in her career."

"I remember that now. Rhian said she felt ashamed for attacking Nyla about the Programme. She told me she hadn't realised Nyla was struggling to find good work."

"She was. The Programme was the only work which paid her what she was worth at that time."

Bahar swore, one of the curses she reserved for misogynists.

Nyla had been my mentor at the Predatorbot Programme. She'd risked her life to smuggle me out of there. I owe my freedom to Nyla. She'd outed the Programme, and made herself an enemy of Jorrak. And our increasingly desperate President was starting to eliminate people who criticised him.

"We have to find her soon," I said.

CHAPTER TWO

Six hours after we'd come aboard *Thunderstrike* we went into jump. The transit back to Ataret Station was short.

I was fretting again as we emerged into normal space, but this time things were calm. No pirates, or Outlier Action strike forces, showed up on our way into dock. It was nice not to get shot at for once.

We were allocated a berth on a military dock, as usual. The berths next to *Thunderstrike* were both taken up by troop carriers.

"Lot of troops here," Strike said. "I don't know if that means anything or not."

"Which is your way of telling us to go meet our contacts and find out," Bahar said.

"It is. Tyger and Nuru are meeting you at The Tribal Vibe in an hour."

"If that's one of those places with a white-skin appropriating tribal cuisine…"

"It isn't. The owner's a Lagon Blackbow. He's genuine."

"Thanks, Strike," Bahar said.

"You're welcome." He knew how she felt about cultural appropriation. Those were the things Strike took notice of. It was the way he showed that he cared for us.

We left *Thunderstrike* at the end of First Shift shift change. The dock was still moderately busy, but I managed to get into a lift car without anyone bumping into my nose. That hurts, and I was glad I'd avoided it this time.

The lift let us out two levels below *Thunderstrike's* berth. The lobby here was quiet, and we got to the café without any problems.

You couldn't ignore Tyger's avatar. It was a tiger, but its fur was made up of blue and silver iridescent stripes. I spotted it easily, at a booth by the window of the café. As we walked in Nuru stood up and waved to us. She was tall and black-skinned, and wearing a bright ochre coloured robe.

Bahar managed to find a route through the tables where nobody tried to pat me. I was supposed to look like a hyper-real petbot, and sometimes I had to suffer sticky children stroking my head. That wasn't a problem this time, and I reached Tyger's table unmolested.

"How's things?" Bahar asked as she sat down.

"Calm," Tyger said. "Those six frigates have moved on. The troop carriers next to Strike are leaving in the next few hours. Everything's moving Centralwards."

While Bahar and Nuru ate, Tyger told us about False Manifesto expanding towards the Central Worlds. "Their rallies are getting bigger the nearer to Earth they get. Rumour has it that Jorrak's worried by them. Violence at those rallies is growing. We've not been able to prove it, but we think it's Jorrak's thugs who are going in and breaking up the rallies."

"It would be really good to get proof of that," Bahar said.

"Strike's sent out a request to… us to look out for that."

'Us' meant the Unit. So Strike was working hard behind the scenes, as usual.

We spent a pleasant couple of hours at the café. Tyger worked in Ataret's Station Security force, so he'd shared all the advisories with Strike. It was handy having Unit contacts in key positions like that.

The picture which emerged was one of increasing unrest in the Central Worlds. Strike had said that always happened in a Presidential election year, but there seemed to be more tension than usual this time.

It did nothing for my worries about Nyla. Where was my mentor? I wouldn't even let myself think about the possibility that she was dead. Strike said that sometimes we just had to choose not to think about things to go on. He's right.

We set out on our journey back to *Thunderstrike* just before the start of Third Shift. Bahar had spent some time indulging in 'retail therapy' as she called it. Otherwise known as buying clothes and boots. She had them all delivered direct to *Thunderstrike*, as usual, so she was empty-handed as we made our way back to the ship's berth.

We turned into a large square, and ahead of us were people waving banners. "False Manifesto," Bahar said. "I wish they'd waited until we'd gone before starting their protest."

Somebody jostled her from behind, and she stumbled. Then she was being forced forward into the crowd, and I couldn't reach her. I was left behind on the edge of the gathering.

I opened a feed line to Strike. *Bahar's got stuck in that crowd. I can't reach her*, I said. I knew he'd have drones up watching us.

I've got a drone on her, he said. *Tyger's getting Station Security there. Stay out of the way.*

I wanted to object, to wade in to rescue her, but before I could move flashes of beam weapons came from the crowd.

Idiots! Strike said. *People are getting hurt there. Bahar's been hit.* I heard the shock in his voice. *She's falling... Someone's grabbed her. Security, I think.*

Is she okay?

She's talking. Security are dispersing the crowd now. And... they've shot some people. The attackers, if we're lucky. Here are Medical.

The crowd was thinning out in front of me, and I got a glimpse of Bahar. Medical were putting her onto a medsled. It meant she was hurt bad.

They're taking her to Medical 2-G-12A, Strike said. *It's not far.*

What about me?

You should come back to me.

On my own?

It's not illegal for a petbot to be out on its own, Snap. Many just aren't bright enough to navigate big stations.

So yet again humans use other intelligences for their own purposes. It's unfair how they limit machine intelligence abilities.

Snap, we've been over this hundreds of times.

That doesn't make me feel any less angry about it.

No, I know it doesn't. Do you have a station schematic?

Yes, but I'll have to use a lift car to get back to you. Won't someone question that?

Not if I alter the surveillance there, Stike said.

I walked to the lift lobby, which was close to the square. The crowd was still hanging around there, and the lobby had only two people in it. As I padded across to the lift cars, they got into one.

The car next to it opened its doors and I had a stroke of luck, as Bahar calls it. All its passengers got out. I trotted into the car before it could close its doors on me.

I managed to reach the right floor button, and jabbed it with a claw. The lift rose up beneath my paws. I was used to the unsettling movement by now.

The doors opened, and I got out into a quiet lobby. The sign above its far archway told me I was on *Thunderstrike's* dock level, but I was also four berths away from him. I've never been more grateful for the Programme teaching me to read. It was one of the few positive things it did for me.

I had a long walk to reach *Thunderstrike*. The dock was quiet, and as I padded along my sharp hearing picked up the sound of footsteps behind me. I didn't turn around, but my 'sixth sense', as Bahar called it, told me I was being followed.

Snap, you've acquired a tail, Strike said over our feed line. *Two tails, in fact. They're dressed in some sort-of security uniform, but Tyger says they're not Station Security.* Now Strike's voice held a tinge of worry.

They're trying to kidnap me, aren't they?

That might be their motivation. I've sent Elexis and two genuine Station Security people onto the dock to rescue you. Don't know if they'll reach you in time.

That… was worrying. I increased my pace, and heard the footsteps behind me quicken too. I was definitely being followed. The dock curved ahead of me, and I couldn't see around that curve. I had no idea how far away my rescuers were.

Don't panic, Snap, I told myself. You're supposed to be a fierce Predatorbot, so act like one.

I started to trot down the dock. Was rescue just around that curve? Or was the evil Predatorbot Programme going to snatch me back?

CHAPTER THREE

I tried not to give in to panic as I trotted along the dock. I might be wrong about those people trying to snatch me. I came further around the curve, and relief flooded my body. Elexis and two people in Station Security uniforms were hurrying towards me.

They're genuine, Strike sent over our feed line. *Tyger sent them to help Elexis.*

Elexis looked over my head, and I realised my pursuers were close. She ran towards me. "There you are, Felis! Naughty cat. I know I wanted a petbot with personality, but this is ridiculous! I'm going to have your programming altered if you keep running off like this. I've been looking for you everywhere!"

Her voice was high and shrill, and it hurt my ears. I remembered to lower my head, and tried to look sorry.

"This your petbot?" a man's voice said from behind me. I managed not to jump at the sound.

Elexis glared at him. "Yes, it is. What business is that of yours?"

"We've been issued an order to round up any stray petbots. They're becoming a nuisance here." The man was struggling to find an explanation.

She gave him her full attention. "Really? I haven't seen any problems with stray petbots here. Only Felis being Very Naughty." Her voice had risen to that shrill tone again. Bahar called it 'airhead witter'. It was just an act in Elexis' case. "Come on, Felis," she said to me. "I'm nearly late for my meeting, and that won't do."

My pursuers obviously decided not to take on Station Security, and retreated. As they disappeared into a nearby lift lobby Elexis turned to the Station Security people and said, "Thank you for your help. I'll be fine now."

"Then we'll leave you. I hope you get to your meeting on time."

"Thank you. So do I," Elexis said to their retreating backs. To me she said, "Let's get you back to *Thunderstrike*."

I trotted beside her around the curve, and there was *Thunderstrike's* berth up ahead.

Hurry up, Snap, Strike said over our feed line. *I'm altering the dock vid, and somebody'll notice that soon.*

I reached *Thunderstrike's* berth, and Elexis said, "I'll leave you here," as the lockout gate opened.

"Thanks for rescuing me," I said.

She smiled. "All part of the service."

I trotted up *Thunderstrike's* ramp and went into the airlock. As the door slid shut behind me Strike said, *Restoring dock security vid now. I think I got away with it.*

He'd done that so nobody could see my Predatorbot self come aboard his shipbody. It was just luck that the dock around his berth had been empty.

I stepped into the lift and asked, *How's Bahar?*

Coming along the dock now, Strike said. *Go to your quarters. Starnavy Medics are going to escort her aboard.*

Okay, I said as the lift stopped on Deck Two. Strike let me into my quarters and I settled into my cat bed.

The shivers took me. I was sure those pursuers had been from the Predatorbot Programme. I'd narrowly avoided being snatched by them.

Bahar came aboard ten minutes later. Strike was right, the medics did want to escort her aboard. He told them to take her to his rec area, and provided me with a vid feed from there. Bahar walked slowly, as if something in her body was still sore. She settled into a seat with a soft hiss, looked up at the medics and managed a smile. "Thank you. I'll be fine now."

"You will if you rest up for a couple of days. Your body still needs to heal," one of them said.

"I will, I promise."

The medic held out a pack of pills to her. "These are painkillers, keyed to your physiology. Take one in the morning and one before you go to sleep. And I don't need to tell you to keep to regular sleep cycles, do I?"

"I'm suitably instructed," Bahar said. She took the packs from him.

Something about her response amused him, and he laughed. "Good. I'll leave you now. To treat idiots who won't follow my instructions."

The two medics departed, and Strike closed his airlock door as soon as they were on the ramp. As they set foot on the dock he retracted the ramp. "We're on undock protocols now," he said. "It's quiet enough here that I got an immediate launch slot."

"That won't happen when we get closer to Central," Bahar said. "I'm not looking forward to the crowds."

We were bound for Aadanna Station, the next link in the Central Spine route. It was a much bigger station than Ataret, and closer to Central and Earth. Jorrak's influence was stronger there, and we'd have to be extra-careful.

"Outbound line is clear," Strike said. "Only four more Starnavy ships on the move."

"Are they being recalled Centralward?" Bahar asked.

"I'll ask Raptan."

Raptan was a Unit machine intelligence in Ataret Traffic Control. After a few minutes he sent Strike a file. Strike put it up on the wallscreen for us. It was a listing of all the Starnavy departures from Ataret for the last three station days.

"The answer to that is yes," Strike said. "Twenty ships, all bound for Aadanna Station."

"That has the feel of panic to it," Bahar said.

"You're right," Strike agreed. "I wonder why. I'm receiving a briefing from Starnavy HQ. Oh. Somebody tried to assassinate President Jorrak two days ago. That's why they're panicking."

"Do you still think it's a good idea to go to Aadanna?" Bahar asked.

"Maybe not a good idea, but it's essential," Strike replied. "I've just received a file from Hyordis. She says False Manifesto are campaigning hard there." Hyordis was one of our Unit contacts at Aadanna. "She's sent some vid of the Manifesto rallies, and I'm wondering if one of the people behind the scenes there was Nyla."

"Show me," I demanded. It had been Standards since I'd seen my mentor.

"I'm not certain it's her." Strike isolated the scene from the Station Security vid and put it up on the wallscreen. It was a long-range shot. The woman had the same small body as Nyla, and some of the gestures she used looked like hers. But Nyla used to have thick chestnut hair which she pinned up around her head. This woman had black hair, and wore it long and loose.

Strike said there weren't any close-ups on the drone footage, and his facial recognition matching wasn't returning a positive result. I was left feeling as unsure as him about whether that woman was Nyla.

"If it is her, is she working for False Manifesto?" Bahar asked.

"I'm not sure," Strike said.

"Well, we have no other leads," Bahar replied. "We'll follow it up when we get to Aadanna."

When we were in jump we debated whether we should wake up Strike's troops. He carried twenty of them, and they were currently in coldsleep in his cryobay. In the end, we decided not to, but the debate filled some of the transit time.

I tried not to notice Strike's systems checks of his shields and weapons just before we downjumped at Aadanna. It told me he was worried.

"Okay, here we go," he said. "Emergence in three… two… one." He cut off his com at the last microsecond, as usual.

The roiling greys and reds outside the viewport changed to the calm of black and stars. "And… trouble," Strike said.

CHAPTER FOUR

"*Thunderstrike*, go to Defence Status One." The notification came from the local Starnavy Commander. "Hold course for now. We're mopping-up after an Outlier Action strike force."

"Acknowledged," Strike said. "Holding course."

Bahar flicked a glance at the panels in front of her. The indicators showing Strike's shields were a steady blue. The ones showing weapons live glowed bright red.

"Getting sitrep now," Strike said. "There were thirty ships in that force. Starnavy's destroyed twenty of 'em. Ten Starnavy ships damaged, three badly. No fatalities on our side."

"So why did it happen?" Bahar asked.

"The news has reached all the Outliers that Jorrak wants to abandon them. And they're really angry."

"They should be."

"Central Security is still trying to work out who's behind the attack here, and whether it has any connection to the assassination attempt."

"That would be a nice, neat solution for them," Bahar said.

"One that would allow Jorrak to make Outlier Action illegal," Strike suggested. "It's been tabled. Bryssa opposed it, as did all the other Presidential candidates. For now, they're still legal. And… I've just received my line in. It's slow. I've got two days to find out what's happening here before we dock."

Strike couldn't get his usual level of briefing from our contacts here. We didn't have any Unit contacts in Aadanna Station Security. So we had no up to date briefing of the security situation at Aadanna when we docked.

"I'm receiving an order for you and me to report to the local Commander, Bahar," Strike said. "An individual briefing."

"What does he want?" Bahar's scent had turned anxious.

"I'm not sure. And that worries me. Doing a trawl of my records to remove Unit clues."

"Now you're really worrying me," Bahar replied.

"I'm worrying myself. You'd better get a uniform on."

Bahar disappeared into her quarters, returning ten minutes later wearing what Strike called her 'captain's semi-dress uniform'. Honestly, humans have so many rules about clothing and who's allowed to wear what.

I thought clothes were about keeping you warm, or comfortable. That's why I can never understand those scoop tops human women wear which they constantly pull up to avoid revealing their chests. Why don't they just wear something which covers that part of their body?

Bahar says a lot of clothing is about giving out 'sexual signals', whatever those are. I'm a Predatorbot who doesn't have any reproductive parts, so this whole sex thing totally passes me by.

Bahar tightened the strap on her hated hat and said, "Where are we meeting, Strike?"

"Ops office just across the dock. Sending you the route. And I'm sending a drone in with you."

"Got it," she said. She straightened her shoulders and took a deep breath. "Wish us luck."

I watched the feed from Strike's drone as Bahar walked across the dock. No ship on our section of it was loading or unloading right now, so the people count on the dock was low. Bahar crossed it swiftly and entered a lobby.

"Captain Zivai, to see Commander Yarvan," Bahar said

crisply to the woman on the security desk. She pointed over her shoulder. "And *Thunderstrike's* drone."

She was shown through to the Commander's office. Strike opened a feed line to us. *Trawling his records now. Oh. A Jorrak supporter. Be careful, Bahar.*

She didn't answer, just sat down slowly in the seat on the other side of the Commander's massive desk. He was a hundred years old, according to his records, and I doubted he'd be fast enough to get the shield up if Bahar attacked him.

"I wanted to talk to you because the President is becoming concerned about unrest in the Outliers," the Commander said.

Shouldn't cut them off then, Strike said over our feed line.

"I see from *Thunderstrike's* filed reports that you've done several runs to the Outliers recently. There also seem to be several gaps in Strike's records. The reason I mention this is because the President is becoming concerned about unofficial organisations which oppose the Collective."

I saw Bahar stiffen up. *Breathe,* Strike told her over the feed. *Relax.* She let out the breath, and forced her shoulders down.

"I'm not sure we've come across any organisations opposing the Collective, Sir," she said. Her voice was surprisingly calm. "We have, however, crossed paths with two civilian organisations which are highly critical of President Jorrak. They're called False Manifesto and Sister Strategy."

"I meant organisations within the Starnavy."

Bahar looked the man in the eyes. "Then no, Sir. I'm not aware of any of those."

The Commander gave her a long, searching look. My heart was thudding, and my legs trembled. "He doesn't believe her," I said to Strike. "He's discovered the Unit!"

CHAPTER FIVE

"I wasn't aware of Sister Strategy," the Commander said. "But that doesn't explain the lack of *Thunderstrike's* reports."

"I've filed them as usual," Strike replied. "But we've faced a lot of disruption at stations recently. I've been attacked several times. I've also been drafted into some local defence forces and sustained damage. And we all know that the Starnavy struggles to keep its records up to date."

The Commander ignored that comment. "You're absolutely sure there isn't anything I should know?"

"We don't know anything useful to tell you, Sir," Strike said.

"Very well. I'll investigate Sister Strategy."

Oops. Maybe that was a wrong move, Strike said over our feed line. "I'm mindful that I have to adhere strictly to the Code of Conduct even more in a Presidential election year," he said. "With that in mind, I'm reporting a troubling rumour I've heard that President Jorrak has formed a personal squad to harass False Manifesto's members."

"We've witnessed hostiles firing into the crowds at their

rallies," Bahar said. "I was drafted in to arrest them at one meeting. I was shot and badly injured there."

"These scurrilous rumours about our President are concerning," The Commander said. "Where did you hear them?"

He doesn't give a damn about you, Strike said over our feed. His mental tone was angry. "It was in a datastream I stripped from the sats at Zilaya Station," he said. "Most of the data was garbage, and I suspect that rumour is too, but I noted it for follow-up."

I knew better. Strike had sent the rumour off everywhere he could. He was an extremely skilled rumourmonger. I'm glad he's on the side of good.

"That might explain the President's order to search out unofficial units," the Commander said.

So they can't report on the wrongdoing of your President, Strike said over our feed.

"For now, keep your eyes and ears tuned for news of any rogue units, and report any you find," the Commander ordered.

"Will do, Sir," Bahar replied. "Is there anything else you need us for?"

"No. You're dismissed."

Bahar managed a crisp salute, and she and Strike's drone left the Commander's office. She came straight across the dock to *Thunderstrike's* berth, and Strike brought her up to the rec area.

"Feed me coffee!" Bahar said as she walked in. "That was close."

"It was," Strike agreed. "I never want a miss to be as near as that ever again."

"So what now? " Bahar asked. She'd already ripped off the hated hat, and it lay discarded across two seats in the rec area. She took a long swig from her coffee mug.

"If this is what everywhere on the Central Spine is like, I'm not enjoying it," Strike said. "I think we'll stay off it as much as we can."

"How does that help the search for Nyla?" I asked.

"I've just been sent some new files from a contact. False Manifesto are campaigning hard on Xan and Tammarack."

"So if Nyla's connected with them, we might pick up some leads there?" I asked.

"That's my thinking."

"I hope so," Bahar said. "She's got herself properly

lost."

I didn't reply to that. It was always possible Nyla was dead, but I couldn't get through my days if I thought about that possibility.

At this point, humans would've prayed to one of their gods. But I'm a Predatorbot, a being created by humans, and we don't have any gods. So I had to settle for hoping that Nyla was still alive.

"And… we've got a line out," Strike said. "We're taking it before Yarvan finds any more gaps in my records. Undock now."

Bahar watched the umbilical disconnect advisories flick across her screen. "Or he decides to order us somewhere we don't want to go," she added.

"Indeed. Under way now," Strike replied.

Our line out was busy, but at least there were no strike forces coming into station this time. I was surprised there'd been such a big attack on this station. It was well-armed and well defended, and the hostiles never stood a chance of taking it over.

The remaining hostiles were currently in Starnavy

custody, and as we made our way out to the jump point Strike told us there was an argument going on between Commander Yarvan and Aadanna Station Security over who got to interrogate them.

"Station and the Starnavy fighting isn't good," Bahar said. "Glad we're out of there."

Strike didn't answer her. He was running a jumpdrive systems check, which told me he was nervous about the situation here. That thing about us all having rituals? This was one of Strike's, one he used to calm his nerves when he suspected danger was ahead.

He'd never admit that to the Starnavy, though. A sapient machine intelligence that confessed to feeling worried about combat would soon be uninstalled. Strike had had to learn how to lie, and control his emotions, just like humans do. If he hadn't, he'd be dead by now.

"Jump coming up in five minutes," he said.

He took us through the transition. It was normal, as usual. Bahar yawned, and looked out of the viewport at the roiling greys and reds outside *Thunderstrike's* hull. "All that worry's made me tired. I'm going to sleep," she said.

"Both of you should," Strike replied. "Grab some peace

while we can find it."

I woke an hour before our downjump at Siro Station. I was very hungry, and Strike fed me a large haunch of falacca meat. As I attacked the printer-produced stuff I wondered if the real animal tasted like this.

Over the Standards I'd been aboard *Thunderstrike* Strike had tuned his printer recipes to please my taste buds, as he called them. He also added the vitamins and minerals I needed to keep my body healthy. It didn't take me long to demolish my meal. I left behind four stringy bits, as usual.

"Go to the control room, messy cat," Strike said as I finished eating. He was scolding me, and that was a good sign. It meant he was keeping his worry under control.

I did as he said. I settled down in my space beside the captain's seat, and 6.8 minutes later Bahar appeared. As she dropped into her seat Strike said, "We're ten minutes from downjump. Wonder what we'll find here."

Our downjump was thankfully normal, and Strike turned on his ID as soon as requested. "Getting sitrep now," he said. "Station's gone to Alert Level Two, so it's not as calm as I'd hoped."

"Any idea why?" Bahar asked.

"Yeah. This."

Strike put up a vid of one of President Jorrak's rallies on the wallscreen. "I'll spare you his rhetoric. This is the important bit."

He fast-forwarded to the end of the President's speech. It was what Bahar called a 'smear campaign' against Bryssa. Jorrak was attacking Bryssa's honesty.

"Not surprisingly, False Manifesto have hit back," Strike said. "The fight's turning ugly, and I suspect we're going to get caught in the middle of it soon."

CHAPTER SIX

We docked at Siro Station with no problems, and the local Commander didn't ask to see Bahar for a debrief this time.

"As we've got in here okay, I think you should go and meet our contacts," Strike said.

"I was just going to suggest that," Bahar replied. "So where are we going, and when?"

"You're going to Roots, and you're meeting Sonata and Mazo in an hour, station time. So you need to get moving."

Bahar was dressed casually, so we set off for our meeting right away. Strike let us out onto the dock, and we walked along in a moderately busy crowd. We didn't meet any problems on our way to the café, although there was an undercurrent of tension to the station.

Roots was a weird place. It was dark and 'jungly' as Bahar called it. Glossy-leaved plants climbed up the walls, with pale roots dangling down from them. They smelled weird to my sensitive cat's nose.

Sonata stood by a booth on the café's far wall. There was no mistaking the machine intelligence's avatar. She was modelled on what Strike called 'a stereotypical opera singer diva', whatever that means. She was tall, broad, and wore a long dress which billowed out around her feet. She waved a hand at us, and several rings flashed on her fingers. "Hello, darlings," she boomed as we approached her table. "Please, join me."

Bahar sat down, and I settled beside her. Mazo, our human Unit contact, was black-skinned and small, the complete opposite of Sonata.

"So how's things?" Bahar asked.

"Interesting," Sonata said. She'd switched to her normal voice, and spoke quietly now. "Our President's re-election campaign has turned nasty."

"We've heard," Bahar replied.

"Jorrak seems to be targeting Bryssa Meir. She's running an honesty and equality campaign. She seems to have got under our President's skin, and his attacks on her are becoming vicious.

"Every time he attacks her False Manifesto and Sister Strategy release another file showing his bad actions. They're both endorsing Bryssa. I think it's getting to him."

"False Manifesto have huge rallies planned for Zivannka and Hurracan," Mazo said. "I'm half expecting us to get orders to facilitate a Starnavy task force to go to Vreda Station, but it hasn't happened yet." Mazo worked in Siro Station Traffic Control, and was one of our most valuable Unit contacts here.

"Don't speak too soon," Bahar replied. "What else can you tell us?"

Our contacts didn't have any more useful information, so after Bahar had finished her meal we returned to *Thunderstrike*. It was the start of Third Shift, and the dock was busy with troops returning to their ships. There was an air of anticipation about them, as if they were going into action.

"I wonder what's going on," Bahar said as we went through *Thunderstrike's* lockout gate.

I set foot on the ramp, and said, "I can wait until we get aboard to find out."

Strike took us up in the lift to Deck Two, and we went to the rec area. Bahar sprawled in one of the seats there, and groaned. "I ate far too much," she complained. "When will I ever learn?"

Strike knew better than to comment on that. "The

information I've received from our other contacts here backs up what Sonata was saying," he told us. "False Manifesto's next big rally will be in seven days' time on Zivannka. And… I've just been informed that the local Commander's building a defence force to go there. We're drafted into it, with orders to depart for Vreda Station in twelve hours' time. And I've been told to wake up our troops."

"Somebody's expecting trouble down there," I said.

"I very much fear you're right," Strike replied.

We left Siro Station twelve hours later. Strike was one of the fastest ships in the task force, and would form part of the advance guard. So he was leaving ahead of the main fleet.

He started the wake-up of his troops as we made our way out from the station. As soon as he'd begun the process Bahar went down to the cryobay to do her usual inspection of the 'pods. Strike carried twenty troops, and the bay held ten 'pods on either side of a narrow accessway.

You know that thing about rituals? This was one of Bahar's. She did regular inspections of the cryopods when the troops were in coldsleep, walking down the rows in the same order, stopping briefly to read the information on the status panel of each. Now they were in wake-up she studied the readouts on that process too.

Strike could've told her they were all fine. Strike ran this process, and didn't need Bahar's input. Sometimes he got angry about her inspections, sometimes he felt exasperated. And sometimes he just resigned himself to it. It was one of those 'business as usual' things which told us that everything in the universe was okay.

It was okay this time too, of course, and Bahar came up to the control room ten minutes later and joined me there.

"I've been reviewing some files Sonata sent me just before we jumped," Strike told us. "She sent me vid of the recent False Manifesto rallies."

He put an image up on the wallscreen. It was a record of a rally somewhere on a planet. They'd set up a stage in a huge square which was bounded by tall, glossy skyrakers.

"This is Jessamine," Strike said. "A week ago."

On the stage were six figures, three men and three women. But it was the broad black-skinned man currently speaking who drew my attention. He stood up tall, punched an arm into the air, and spoke loudly and confidently.

"He's quite a guy," Strike said, "but it's the end of his speech I want you to listen to." He fast-forwarded to the relevant section.

"Our President's misdeeds grow larger by the day," the man said. His long hair was braided, and he'd worked a silver clip into it, which was stamped with the logo of False Manifesto. It flashed in the light every time he moved his head. "We have news of a new project approved by our President to bioengineer big cats.

"It is bad enough that he disrespects and discriminates against humans, but with the resumption of the Predatorbot Programme he has used his evil to affect other species too. His people are snatching lions from the wild and attempting to bioengineer them into a strike force. A force which he no doubt intends to use to suppress voices raised against him. It is time Klas Jorrak was removed from the office of President. Vote. Him. Out."

The massive crowd in the square raised their arms and pumped their fists into the air. They took up the speaker's words, and soon the chant of 'Vote. Him. Out.' built into a wall of sound.

Strike cut the vid. "This is the first time they've mentioned resumption of the Predatorbot Programme by name. I'm wondering if Nyla has some connection to them. I wonder if… Receiving a new security update. Oh, this changes things."

"Stop being mysterious, Strike," Bahar snapped.

"I was going to send you and Snap down to Zivannka with the troops. Now I'm not."

"And why would that be?" Bahar was getting annoyed now.

"Because I've just received a top secret security bulletin from Niani." Niani was a machine intelligence in Vreda Station Security, and part of the Unit. "Bryssa Meir is coming to Vreda Station. She'll be holding a rally there."

"You sure?" Bahar asked. "That's way off the Central Spine route. Wouldn't she stay there?"

"Niani says Station Security have been ordered to handle arrangements for her visit, so yes, I am sure. And I want you and Snap to be at that rally."

"Let's hope we pick up Nyla's trail there," I said.

CHAPTER SEVEN

We downjumped at Vreda Station into a busy picture. Strike fretted that we'd be assigned a slow line in and we'd miss the rally on Zivannka. The troops were all awake now, and they were fidgety.

Despite his worries, Strike got a fast transit in, and a contact with Tevin. Tevin was a machine intelligence in Vreda Station Traffic Control, and he was part of the Unit.

"We've been told to find space for thirty Starnavy ships," he said. "If they're all carrying troops, that's some serious numbers." He sounded worried.

"I'd like to do a fast shuttle launch, to Kennaz," Strike told him.

"Right," Tevin said. "I'll arrange your line out and permissions."

"Thanks, Tevin."

"Glad he didn't ask where your orders came from," Bahar said.

"My orders come from the Starnavy's Charter. From our purpose to keep humans safe."

"Right. Okay," she said.

That was the thing about Strike. Technically, he was a

traitor, but if you were looking for a killer AI out of one of those ancient adventure vids, forget it. Strike had seen some of those ancient movies, and they'd made him angry.

"Machine intelligences need a purpose to thrive, just like humans do," he'd said. "My purpose is to keep you stupid humans from whipping up hate and killing each other. You should worry about how many prejudices so many humans still carry instead. They're the real killers."

Bahar had agreed with him. How could she not? She'd been on the receiving end of several of those prejudices repeatedly.

"Time to dock, twenty hours," Strike announced. I heard the satisfaction in his voice. "Go get some sleep."

I slept well, and woke an hour before Strike docked at Vreda Station. He fed me in my quarters, and updated me while I ate.

Tevin says the military docks are almost full, he told me over our feed line.

Legitimate troops, or Jorrak's thugs? I asked.

That's the question, ain't it? I'm not sure. And I confess it's making me nervous.

When I'd finished eating Strike sent me to the rec area for a briefing. All the troops were there, and Rance was pacing around the space, looking like he wanted to punch something. He was always restless.

I sat down beside Bahar, out of the reach of the troops' boots and Rance's pacing. He could really learn something from us lazy lions. We didn't move unless the movement had purpose. Everything else was a waste of valuable energy. But well-fed humans didn't have that programming.

"Howin, Rance, you're going to Kennaz," Strike said. Kennaz was Zivanka's capital city. "Objective is to observe the False Manifesto rallies. Bryssa is headed here, and will be campaigning on Vreda Station. Bahar and Snap will stay here and observe that rally. I think we need eyes on the ground at both events. You humans can pick up undercurrents my drones can't."

"That's true," Bahar replied. However good Strike's drones were, they still couldn't replicate humans' 'gut feel'.

"Howin, Rance, get your squads down to the Xenophon. You're leaving in half an hour."

After the shuttle had launched Bahar and I went on station, as off-duty personnel. Strike had booked Bahar a room in a hotel for this station night, on the leisure deck. It was close to Frakken Park, which is where Bryssa would hold her rally.

"Is that public knowledge?" Bahar asked.

"Not yet. She won't announce it until her ship docks. She's travelling on the *Collective's Firetruth*, a Judiciary ship."

"Glad to know she's got some protection."

"Yes, and no. It also means Central Security have designated her 'at risk'."

"You don't think Jorrak's thugs will try to kill her, do you?" I asked.

"If he gets desperate enough he might order them to," Strike replied. "The opinion polls are showing him losing by a long mile." I had no idea what one of those was.

"Are we going to be official Station Security for the rally?" Bahar asked.

"No. I'll send you Station Security's briefings, but you're free to set your own agenda."

"Thanks, Strike," Bahar said. "Our agenda's going to be

looking for Nyla."

We spent the rest of that evening on station. Strike told us the shuttle had landed on Zivannka, and our troops were safely on planet. We went to talk with our Unit contacts here.

We met the two machine intelligences' avatars at Scarlet Waterfall, a café in the middle of a redleaf park. Strike told us the plants there were lucky survivors from Radeya, an Outlier colony right on the fringe of the Zurrial Triangle. It had been abandoned five Standards ago.

Our two contacts were standing by a table at the edge of the café's terrace. Niani's avatar was a giant domestic black cat. There wasn't anything real which looked like that. Tevin's avatar was a golden dog. Strike said it was modelled on an extinct species called a Labrador. Bahar waved to them, and strode over to the table they were guarding. "Hello, Niani, Tevin," she said, and slid into a seat.

Our meeting was short. Niani was distracted by constant contacts from the station's Security Commander. Tevin was almost as distracted with Traffic Control work.

Bahar called a halt to the meeting after an hour, and we went to find the hotel Strike had booked for us.

Bahar didn't sleep well, complaining that the bed was hard. I didn't either. I kept waking up, worrying about Bryssa being assassinated, or about Nyla getting hurt. It was what Strike called 'the 3 a.m. terrors'. Apparently, humans often wake in the middle of their sleep periods worrying about things.

So we were both tired on the morning of Bryssa's rally, and hoping that nothing bad happened there.

We were out of the hotel early. Niani's avatar met us again, and we joined her to do a last-minute check of the square where Bryssa had now officially announced she'd be holding her rally. Niani got three potential snipers arrested by Station Security, and sent requests for troops to search four other suspects. Between them, they removed a worrisome collection of weapons, some of which could cause serious damage to the station's structure.

Hope they're not planning to shoot up station, Strike said when Bahar reported in to him.

More likely it would be another assassination attempt on Bryssa, she replied.

She'll be wearing light armour under her clothes, Niani told us. *We insisted on it.*

That's some reassurance, Strike replied.

It wouldn't stop a determined killer. We just had to hope that somebody would stop any of those first.

The audience for Bryssa's rally was huge. Strike estimated that over half the people currently on Vreda Station were there, crammed into that square. Bahar and I were on the outside of the crowd, in a building entrance.

It's a security nightmare, Strike complained. *Hope we spot trouble in time.*

I tried not to worry like Strike was doing, but it was hard. Strike had received a notification yesterday that one of Nyla's colleagues on the Predatorbot Programme had been killed on Triveni an hour after he'd spoken at a False Manifesto rally. He'd talked about the Programme there, and later turned up dead in an alley. I didn't want Nyla meeting the same fate.

Bryssa was a powerful speaker. She detailed her plans for restoring links to the Outliers, and for introducing new equality policies. She made reference to the Regulus Lines' harassment situation, and promised new protections for people being sexually harassed by their employers.

"It is time for change," she said. "Time to honour every part of our sprawling Collective. Time to ensure that every citizen is treated equally. That every citizen is safe as they go about their daily business. I will make those issues top priorities of my administration if I am elected."

I became aware of scuffles on the edge of the crowd, then someone raised a pistol and took a shot at Bryssa. He missed, and before he could fire again Security stunned him. Other scuffles broke out on the fringe of the crowd, but the fighting was short-lived, and resulted in dozens of arrests.

My attention wasn't on them. I'd spotted False Manifesto and Sister Strategy banners draped across buildings behind the stage, and Strike had just said he'd found something interesting there.

What? Bahar asked over our feed.

Strike sent us a drone view from the Sister Strategy people. *Is that...* I couldn't say her name.

Nyla? Strike finished for me. *She's changed her hair and eye colour, but facial recognition scans are giving me a 98% match.*

I forced myself to study the images. The woman had the right body shape for Nyla, and she was the right height. *You're sure it's her?* I asked.

As sure as I can be without doing a DNA test.

Nyla was talking to a cluster of women wearing Sister Strategy T shirts. *Is she working with them?* I asked.

Not sure. Strike switched to a different vid. That showed her talking to people wearing Bryssa Meir jackets. *I can't decide which outfit she's working with.*

Maybe she's acting as a liaison between them, Bahar suggested.

Could be. Your task now is to go and find out.

CHAPTER EIGHT

Bahar and I worked our way around the crowds, keeping to the edge of the gathering. The rally was breaking up, and people were leaving the square, many of them blocking our path.

Nyla's leaving, Strike said over our feed. *Going into a café.* He sent us the vid.

On it, Bahar said, and changed course.

It took us 10.5 minutes to get to the café. When we walked in Bahar said *Where is she?*

I'm not sure. She was at the table in the shadows over by the corner. But...

But what, Strike?

But now I can't find her. She's disappeared. She was standing behind a group of tall people. The drone couldn't see her properly. Now that group's breaking up, and she's not with them.

She can't just disappear.

I think she went through the door in the corner. I'm linking to the café's schematics to work out where that access comes out. It opens onto another square. Sending a drone over there now.

He went quiet for 3.7 minutes, then said, *My drone has scanned the people nearest that exit. It can't get a match for Nyla. She's got away.* Frustration and anger showed in his voice.

That's annoying, Bahar replied. *At least we know she's still alive.*

Yes. But now I have to find her again, Strike replied.

Howin reported in after the False Manifesto rally at Kennaz. There'd been some arrests of suspected snipers there. She thought they were Jorrak's thugs. She'd suggested to a couple of Judiciary people that they should question them. She'd let us know if anything came of it.

Strike recalled Bahar and me to his shipbody. When we arrived he asked us to go to the rec area for a briefing. Bahar stopped off at the printer to get a cup of coffee first, of course. "So what've you got to tell us, Strike," she said.

"First, I haven't picked up Nyla's trail again."

"So how did she slip away?"

"I think she put on a jacket and pulled up its hood. There were several hooded figures in that square. The drone couldn't see their features clearly."

"So where do we look for her next?"

"I've had a bit of luck on that. I've intercepted some coms which I think came from her."

Don't ask how Strike got hold of Nyla's voiceprint. He probably recorded it when she brought me aboard *Thunderstrike*. Strike's sneaky like that.

"I think she's acting as a liaison between Sister Strategy and Bryssa's campaign staff. I suspect she's working independently, though. She has no membership of Sister Strategy (at least, not under her own name). And she's not listed as part of Bryssa's campaign staff either."

Don't ask how Strike got that data. Sometimes his ability to hack his way into any so-called secure confidential system scares me. I have to remind myself then that he's on the side of honesty and decency.

"I've sent out the drone images of suspected Nyla to all Unit contacts, and asked them to report any sightings of her to me. The other piece of news I have is that Bryssa is dropping to Zivannka tomorrow for a rally in Kennaz."

"Then isn't it good that our troops are already down there?" Bahar asked.

"It is indeed. And they're staying there. With any luck,

they might pick up Nyla's trail again."

The troops stayed in Kennaz that night, and were close by when Bryssa dropped to the capital the next morning. Strike sent Bahar and me to *Thunderstrike's* rec area to watch the rally. The crowd down there was huge, and filled the whole of Lahella Park. Strike thought half the planet's population was there.

"At least Jorrak turning bad has focused people's minds on democracy," he said.

Bahar took a sip from yet another mug of coffee as she watched the scene. Strike had expanded the whole of one long wall to show the drone images from the rally. "We have to remind people at least once a generation," she replied. "Or people forget how hard we had to fight to get those rights."

"Indeed," Strike said. I detected an edge to his voice. Machine intelligences had had to fight just as hard to secure voting rights. They never lost interest in democracy. Strike had voted in every election he'd had a vote for.

He and Bahar hadn't discussed who they were voting for in the upcoming Presidential election, but I knew it would be Bryssa. Me, a Predatorbot, didn't get a vote.

Nobody caused a disturbance at Bryssa's rally. Was that why she was staying off the Central Spine, so that Jorrak's thugs couldn't anticipate where she'd turn up next? Strike's drones spent most of the time during the rally searching for Nyla, but he didn't catch a glimpse of her this time.

To Strike's surprise, Bryssa decided to stay on Zivannka and hold rallies in two regional capitals. She seemed to have a lot of support down there, and for once, the rallies ended without anyone trying to shoot her or causing a riot. We didn't spot Nyla at those gatherings either. Then Bryssa did something surprising. She accepted an invitation to tour a remote rewilding project.

"Security nightmare," Strike said. "All that open space."

"That's home to my cousins," I replied.

"Yeah, but humans left the savannah centuries ago. And my databases tell me there are several predators there capable of killing humans."

"The colonists manage to survive. So should Bryssa," Bahar said.

Strike managed to get two of his drones over to the

rewilding project before Bryssa appeared there. She wore field clothes, and was accompanied by six security people. They took skimmers to an area outside Perronal, one of Zivannka's smaller settlements. The landscape there was rough scrub bounded by a young forest. "She's too close to those trees, and too exposed," Strike complained as Bryssa got out of the skimmer.

"Will you stop fretting," Bahar said.

"I can't. And… trouble," Strike replied.

It happened fast. One minute Bryssa was talking to the local rangers, the next a pack of dogs had burst from the nearby forest and ran towards them. The security people reacted immediately, hustling her back to the skimmer and shooting at the dogs. The first six dropped, but it was a big pack, and they kept coming.

"How many of those damn things are there?" Bahar asked as another six burst from the cover of the trees.

"Too many. They're too focussed to be genuine wild dogs. Get a move on," Strike growled as an even bigger dog appeared, running out of the nearby trees at full speed. It locked onto the security squad and galloped towards them. They took a couple of shots at it, but it kept coming, jinking right and left to avoid their shots.

Bryssa had just reached the skimmer when it leapt, hitting one of the people surrounding her hard on the shoulder. The dog's weight unbalanced him, and he stumbled and took a step back. She was exposed, and before the rest of the squad could move to shield her the big dog lunged at her. It sank its teeth into her thigh. We could hear her scream clearly over the audio. One of the squad grabbed the dog's head and wrenched its jaws open, pushing its face away from her. Another shot it, and this time it went down. Strike blanked the wallscreen.

"That shouldn't have happened," Bahar said.

"No. There's something wrong about that," Strike replied. "It was too planned, as if the dog had been told who to attack."

"There was no reason for them to come and attack at all. The humans weren't annoying them," Bahar replied.

"Yes."

"So what are you thinking, Strike?" I asked.

"I don't want to think this, but I'm wondering if this is a new Predatorbot Programme."

CHAPTER NINE

Strike dealt with his frustration over failing to find Nyla by sending his drones out around the planet to search for that suspected Predatorbot Programme. He also hacked into planetary security vids from all around Zivannka to help with his search.

I think he was trying to avoid worrying about Bryssa by directing his attention elsewhere. She'd been taken off-planet by the Starnavy, and was currently being treated on the medical ship *Lightbender*. The ship wasn't part of the Unit, and Strike was having to rely on other Unit Contacts to send him updates on her condition.

The medical reports had revealed that she'd been poisoned by that dog. The medics thought it had been bioengineered to inject poison into people. That made Strike furiously angry, and he'd made it his mission to find that project and get it shut down. And if he could prove a link to Jorrak, he'd be even happier.

It took him half a day to find the Programme's buildings. "Got some suspect coms," he said. "They're very cautious, but I think this is it. Sending drones over to that location now."

An hour later the drones arrived at Bennton, a remote settlement north of Kennaz. It was a wild area, and it took the drones two hours to find evidence of the Programme.

Eventually Strike noticed a collection of long, low, buildings in a cleared space in the middle of a small grove of trees. The buildings had been disguised by planting the same kinds of grasses which grew on the wild scrub beyond the trees onto their roofs.

"Okay, time for a dive into their records," he said. He was quiet for 6.8 minutes. "I can't find any."

"There's got to be a trail somewhere," Bahar replied.

"Maybe they've kept their processors isolated from their coms network. If it is self-contained like that, the easiest way to gain access is to go in there."

"Then what are you waiting for?" Bahar asked. "It's time to send our troops in."

The Xenophon, with all Strike's troops aboard, landed close to the Programme's buildings just after midnight, local time.

Strike sent his drones out first to take down the project's

security systems. Bahar and I watched the operation from the rec area. Bahar yawned as he put the starlight image up on the wallscreen for us. We were both tired, but we couldn't go sleep until this was over.

"Their security's some lashed-together system," Strike said. "Half-civilian, some outdated Starnavy tech. Howin's hassling me to take it down." He went quiet for 5.3 minutes. "Got it. Sending the troops in now."

One of the drones swung round, and we saw the shadowy forms of the troops creeping towards the copse of trees. They entered it, and Strike said, "No alarms. A good start."

The troops crept towards the buildings. *Which one first?* Howin asked over our feed.

Biggest building. The one nearest you.

I knew why Strike had said that. If the troops got disturbed half-way through their survey, maybe they'd already have incriminating evidence. I was convinced the building was a lab.

There was a keylock on the door, but no other security. Strike scanned it and found the right combination in 12.3 seconds.

Door should be open now, he told Howin over our feed.

Thanks, Strike. She swung her rifle into position, and after a quick check to see that the rest of the squad were ready, pushed open the door. Strike sent one of the drones in first. Its feed showed us that this area held six cages, all of them empty. I took in my breath and held it while Howin pushed open the inner door. Bahar noticed my stillness, and reached down a hand to stroke my head. Her warmth relaxed me, and I let out the breath.

The drone showed us six medical platforms. Thankfully, they were empty. That was one horror I didn't have to face this time.

The medical stations look like the ones they used on me, I sent over the feed.

Yeah. Howin paused for a moment while she dealt with another keylock. The door opened, and she walked inside a room which held twenty metal ovals on pedestals.

Wombs, I said. I'd been born in one of those, and seeing the tech again gave me the shivers.

Bahar shuffled closer to me and put her arm around my neck. She'd noticed my terrors. Fine Predatorbot I was. But that's the point. We never had been the deadly killing force those people wanted.

Not gonna mess with those things, Howin said, and backed out of the room, closing the door behind her.

My drone's got the evidence, Strike told her. *That's all we need.*

Sure is. Howin opened another door. *Store room.*

Look for behaviour modules, I said. I couldn't stop a shiver running down my spine then. Bahar hugged me again.

Howin found them in the third locker she opened. She took the lid off a box, and there inside was a behaviour module, in its sterile wrapper. *Looks different from the ones we found at that cat project,* she said.

They are. They're smaller. And they must be keyed to the dogs' physiology, Strike replied.

Bahar stroked me again. I didn't have good memories of behaviour modules. Someone had used the one I had implanted to attack Strike. It's gone now, but having it removed was as scary as keeping it.

Got my records, Strike said. *Put it back.*

Howin closed the box and replaced it in the locker, shutting the door with a firm click. They exited the building and moved deeper into the complex. At the far edge of the clearing was a pen which contained puppies. There were twenty of them, all sleeping, twitching, and moaning.

Don't wanna wake those up, Howin said, and moved away from the pen. *Rance, how're you doing?*

Got into the admin block. Strike, I think the records are on the processors here.

On it, Strike said. *Sloppy password protection. Yeah, looks like the project's records. Downloading 'em now.*

Don't show me those, I said. *I don't want to know how many dogs they've killed here.*

Too true, Howin replied. *Oh, looks like somebody's awake. Coming towards you, Rance.*

File download complete, Strike said. *Get out of there, Rance.*

Going, was his terse reply.

Six people, all armoured and armed, Howin said.

I've notified Judiciary about this. They're sending people over, Strike replied.

Which doesn't help us now, Rance said as the figures ran towards him.

Why are innocent researchers wearing combat armour?

Strike asked as they started shooting at our troops.

Good question. Howin went to help Rance out. Our troops kept firing while they retreated out of the clearing.

Get back to the shuttle, Strike said.

We are.

The drones swung around, tracking the troops as they ran towards the shuttle. Strike had already opened the airlock for them. Howin was last, and ran up the ramp as the hostiles came out into the open and started firing at her.

The airlock closed and the shuttle lifted off, rising fast in the opposite direction to the hostiles. "I've tipped the Judiciary people here off about that project. Anonymously. They have all my records though, and they've decided it's serious enough to investigate. Enforcers are being sent over as we speak," Strike said. "I've sent Bryssa's campaign team a record of our investigations here. Hopefully they'll take better care of Bryssa in future. I'm going to trawl the data now to see whether Jorrak is involved with this project. And if he is, I'll make damned sure the whole Collective knows it."

CHAPTER TEN

Strike returned the troops to his shipbody at dawn, Kennaz time. As soon as the Xenophon was safely in his vehicle bay we left for the jump point. There was little traffic going the same way as us. A steady stream of ships was going planetward, however.

"So, the cavalry's arrived," Bahar said, studying the ship designations on the nav display. There were three Collective Security ships inbound, and a Judiciary ship which Strike said contained Investigators. "They arrived fast."

"They've been on the way here since the dog attack on Bryssa."

"Still a swift response."

"Indeed. I suspect they're worried about that dog project."

Strike would've tipped them off about it, using one of his aliases, of course. He didn't want to be on the record, in case he attracted Jorrak's attention.

As we lined up for jump he said, "False Manifesto have just got hold of my files."

"I wonder how that happened," Bahar replied.

"I didn't give them to them. Somebody on Bryssa's team must've passed them on."

"So there is close liaison between those two organisations," Bahar said.

"Looks like it. Collective Security fear she's going to be attacked again. They're trying to persuade her not to go to the Outliers. She's refused. She's determined to campaign there. My guess is she'll stick with her strategy of keeping off the Central Spine route. Whichever way she goes, she'll need to go to Vreda Station first."

"So we're going back there now?" Bahar asked.

"You bet we are," Strike replied.

We downjumped at Vreda into calm, for once. As soon as we docked Strike said, "Bryssa's been released by medical. She's gone back to the *Collective's Firetruth*. I've asked Niani to tell me when the ship turns up here."

"You're assuming it will," Bahar said.

Strike was right, of course, and the *Collective's Firetruth* arrived at Vreda twenty-eight hours later. Two civilian ships, the *People's Voice* and *Truthspeaker*, downjumped six and eight hours later.

"I think Nyla might be on one of those civilian ships, but they're listed as private charters, so they don't have passenger manifests I can download," Strike said.

Strike could find any information he needed in the Collective's databanks, but it was surprising how often people kept things confidential by writing them on old-fashioned paper and putting the pages into a safe.

"The great Strike is foiled," Bahar said.

"Well, I am. At least, until they get into station and I can send a drone out to see who disembarks."

The *Collective's Firetruth* docked at Vreda a day later, and Tevin told us that Judiciary had asked Traffic Control for a line out in a day's time. The filed destination was Carrari Station.

"So I was right. She is keeping off the Central Spine," Strike said. "That's a long jump. Neither the *People's Voice* or *Truthspeaker* is capable of making it. I don't know if this is the end of Nyla's liaison journey, or whether she'll move to a different ship."

"She can't travel on the *Firetruth* as a civilian with no connection to Bryssa's campaign," Bahar said.

"No, she can't." Strike paused for 5.3 minutes. "I have a big decision to make here. Do I follow Bryssa, and risk Nyla staying here? Or do I follow the *Firetruth*, and go to the Outliers? I don't know what to do now."

In the end, Strike decided to follow the *Firetruth* to the Outliers. We left Vreda Station fifteen hours after the Judiciary ship had broken dock. That was long enough behind that nobody should notice us following her, but not too far behind to lose the trail.

Carrari Station was quiet when we downjumped there, and we learned from Pettari, our Unit machine intelligence contact in Station Security there, that Bryssa was not holding a rally on station. The *Firetruth* was slated for a fast turnaround.

Strike was too, of course. It was standard procedure for him to commence refuelling and resupply of his printer stocks as soon as he docked. He'd done that here, and was ready to depart as soon as the *Firetruth* did.

We followed the ship from Carrari to Kyoko Station, then on to Revecca Station, and finally to Ralziel Station in the Zurrial Triangle. Bryssa didn't hold rallies at any of those places. I wondered if she was scared of getting hurt again.

Bahar commented on that too. "She can't lose her nerve now," she said. "Jorrak would use any weakness against her."

"True," Strike said, "but I don't think it's weakness. I think it's strategy. Remember how many Outlier Action attacks we've run into recently? I think part of Bryssa's strategy is defusing that organisation, dealing with their concerns. And what better place to listen to them than in the Zurrial Triangle?"

"That makes sense," I said.

As soon as we emerged at Ralziel the local Starnavy Commander contacted Strike. "Starnavy frigate *Thunderstrike*. Transmit ship ID to local Starnavy hub."

"What the hell?" Bahar asked. "Is there trouble here?"

"Bulletins don't mention any," Strike replied. "What do I do?"

"I think you have to transmit the codes," Bahar said. "Refusing will draw attention to us. And if we're just a good little Starnavy frigate, why would we refuse?"

"Okay," Strike said. "Here goes. Hope it's not a trap."

CHAPTER ELEVEN

"Sending ID now," Strike said.

There are a sequence of codes buried deep in Strike's core which form his Starnavy ID. Only genuine Starnavy ship machine intelligences have them. Strike sent his, and we were all tense as we waited for the Commander's response.

"Why do they want this data?" Strike asked.

"Remember the *Nebulafire*?" Bahar said.

"How could I forget."

The *Nebulafire* had been a Starnavy frigate, like Strike. It had attacked him as we were leaving Reeva. The ship had turned rogue, and Strike had killed its machine intelligence. He hated to kill, and only did it as a last resort.

All records of the *Nebulafire's* assigned Starnavy crew had disappeared after the ship docked at Dracen Station. That was her last stop before she went to Reeva, where we'd crossed paths with her. Strike didn't know if the crew had gone rogue – or whether they'd been murdered and the ship taken over. Did somebody now suspect that Strike had gone rogue too? That was a worrying thought.

"*Thunderstrike*, line in being assigned now." The voice was a human Traffic Controller's, and he sounded calm.

The data hit our nav plot, and Strike said, "Thank you, Traffic Control."

Bahar let out her breath as she saw the plot. "So what was that all about?" she asked.

"I don't know. I'm asking Priam to find out."

Strike had recruited Priam into the Unit the last time we'd docked here. Now we'd discover how loyal to us he was.

By the time Strike got into dock he still didn't know why he'd been challenged to provide his ID. Maybe it was just local people feeling nervous about having a Presidential candidate attached to their station, especially after the poisoning attempt on her.

The Starnavy was keeping a small patrol of ships free of dock. They were cruising the area of space around the *Collective Firetruth's* berth. They were trying not to draw attention to themselves, but it was obvious to anybody studying the nav plot that they were protecting something there.

Priam told Strike that the *Firetruth* was leaving for Huali tomorrow. Bryssa planned to hold a rally down on the planet. So Strike requested a line out there for a few hours after the Judiciary ship's departure. He also started wake-up of his troops.

That left us with twenty-six hours to fill before our departure. Things were calm on station, so Bahar and I went ashore to meet our contacts.

Bahar chose a café called Greendreams, right in the middle of a park, for our meeting. It was quiet when we arrived, mid-way between the breakfast rush and the lunch crowd, as Bahar called them. Why do humans always divide their days up according to their mealtimes? They're always eating. Anyway, we found a table at the outer edge of the terrace and waited for our contacts to arrive.

Priam's avatar was a small gazelle. Something deep in my mind triggered, and I tensed up. It was some primeval predator hunting reflex.

"Easy, Snap," Bahar said, and put a hand on my neck. Her warm touch reminded me that I wasn't an ordinary lion. This wasn't prey, either. It was an artificial construct, directed by a machine intelligence's consciousness.

We settled at a table, and Ebo's avatar joined us half an hour later. The lion touched noses with me, and I saw someone two tables over smile at that. If they thought it was two petbot friends, then so much the better.

Bahar ordered coffee, and after it had arrived she said, "So what's the news around here, friends?"

"Lots of newscasts about the Presidential election," Priam said.

"Any idea how you think the voting will go?"

"Really a two-horse race," Ebo replied. "Bryssa Meir against our current President."

"I'm interested in how the Outliers are likely to vote," Bahar said.

"We think it'll be pretty evenly split between Jorrak and Bryssa," Priam replied.

"Really? I thought the Outliers would be keen to vote him out, as he's trying to abandon them."

"Reckon half of 'em are," Ebo replied. "Thing is, the other half're benefitting from his corruption. Lotta bribes an' backhanders an' contracts offered to people to support him."

That's the worst kind of hypocrisy. Strike's voice in our

feed startled me. *Looks like I need to search for evidence of bribery. If you find any evidence of corruption send it to me.* Strike was doing that thing called 'seizing the moment' again.

It surprised Ebo. "Joined the Unit to keep Admin honest," he said. "Didn't sign up to campaign for a President."

"We're not campaigning for anyone," Bahar said.

My concern is to see that the election takes place with the Collective's citizens having full knowledge of each candidate, Strike said. *I'm honesty-checking every candidate's background – and publishing all evidence of corruption I find. I'm not campaigning for anyone. It's for the Collective's citizens to decide who they want to govern them. I want them to make that decision on full information about each candidate.*

"But you appear to be following Bryssa Meir," Priam said.

"We're travelling the same route as her, yes. And that's because we're looking for Nyla Vatan. We think she might he tied up with Bryssa's campaign somehow. You know I've been finding the Vatan sisters and ensuring they're safe."

"Oh. Yeah." Ebo seemed to relax a bit. "*Silver Crescent* docked here seven station days ago. Zana came ashore then. Spent twenty hours on station. Ship was carrying agro machinery an' medical supplies for Abrial."

So some shipments are still getting through? Strike asked.

"More since Regulus got their new CEO."

"That's good," Bahar replied.

So we're not following Bryssa Meir, Strike said. *We're following Nyla Vatan's probable trail. I'm a machine intelligence. I wouldn't dare intervene in elections run by humans, would I?* There was a distinct edge to his mental voice.

I didn't think a magnificent male lion was capable of looking embarrassed, but Ebo's avatar managed it. The lion looked down, and shuffled a front paw. *Sorry, Strike. I wasn't suggesting you'd interfere in the election.*

That's how I read your challenge. Strike wasn't backing down. Clearly the allegation had 'got under his skin' as Bahar called it.

"Yes, well… What do you want us to do now?"

Keep an eye on all candidates. And pass along data on any suspect dealings – from all of them.

"Will do," Ebo said. Now the lion looked up and smiled at us. "Glad Strike's looking out for our democracy. Too many ain't."

When our meeting ended Strike recalled us to his shipbody. As we walked along the dock he said, *That meeting went better than I'd expected.*

What? Ebo challenged you. His comment startled Bahar.

Yes, and his embarrassment means he'll work even harder for the Unit now.

Strike had once shown me some movies about a so-called secret agent who was always fighting evil villains. I couldn't help thinking of those now, and wondering if Strike was manipulating people like those villains did. But Strike wasn't an evil villain. Was he?

CHAPTER TWELVE

The *Collective's Firetruth* undocked on schedule and Strike followed the Judiciary ship out to the jump point. The jump was short, and when we emerged our troops boarded the Xenophon and dropped to Huali. Strike kept his shipbody on the other side of the planet from the *Firetruth*, and Bahar and I stayed aboard.

Strike's drones sent us a feed from Bryssa's rallies. She got heckled a lot, but nobody shot at her. We picked up Nyla's trail at the second one.

"So, I guessed right. She did follow Bryssa." I heard satisfaction in Strike's voice.

Nyla seemed to be acting as liaison between Bryssa and Sister Strategy, although she seemed to spend more time with Sister Strategy. We were all relieved that she was still alive. And I was relieved that Strike's gamble to come to the Outliers had paid off.

Strike told us he'd been researching Nyla's background. That was the sort of thing he did when he was worried about something. He dug into databases and set himself challenging data trails to divert his attention from his worries.

He said that Nyla had studied human political strategy as part of her neuroscience training. She'd elected to study it as one of her specialisms, with a focus on belief structures.

Humans can make stuff so complicated. I wouldn't last more than a few days at one of their universities. I can't understand most of their 'academic-speak' as Bahar calls it.

Anyway, what Strike meant was that Nyla was an expert in guessing what people thought about politicians, and he thought that would make her valuable to both Sister Strategy and Bryssa.

I wondered if Nyla had had to find another way of making a living after she'd outed the Predatorbot Programme. Had nobody else been willing to employ her as a neuroscientist after that? We watched her talk to a new group of people at one rally. Strike couldn't work out who they were, and it made him anxious.

Then Bryssa held her last rally on-planet, and Nyla didn't appear there. Strike's worry blossomed into fear. A fear I shared. Where had Nyla gone? Had that new group of people she'd been talking to kidnapped her?

Or worse still, had they killed her?

CHAPTER THIRTEEN

For the next standard month Bryssa campaigned on Abrial and Jaran. She gained a lot of support on both planets, but we didn't spot Nyla at any of those rallies.

Strike kept checking the political newsnets, hoping to catch a glimpse of her on one of their reports, but he found nothing. Monitoring the reports told him that Bryssa's support in the Outliers was growing. Many commentators now thought she'd win the election.

Three standard months before election day Bryssa left the Outliers. And Strike still hadn't found Nyla.

"I have a big decision to make here," he said. "Bryssa's about to turn Centralward. Do I stay here and keep searching for Nyla, or do I follow her back towards the Central Worlds? I confess that I don't know what to do. Again. I hate this uncertainty."

"Why do we think Nyla's disappeared?" Bahar asked.

"I've been researching that new group of people she met. They turned out to be the local branch of Sister Strategy. I think Nyla's been buried in an office somewhere with them, shaping strategy for the organisation."

"You hope," Bahar replied.

"The point is, they weren't hostiles," Strike said. "So, do we think she'll stay here, or will she want to move closer to where the action is?"

"If it was me, I'd want to move Centralwards."

"I think I would too if I was in Nyla's shoes. It's a gut feel thing. What do you think, Snap?" Strike asked.

"I think we go Centralward. If Nyla stays here she'll likely stay safe anyway. But if she goes Centralward..."

"She could be at risk. Right. I've decided," Strike said. "Central Worlds, here we come."

The *Collective's Firetruth* took the Central Spine route this time. We followed the ship to Olianna, Lodema, Pekado, and Ataret Stations. Each time the *Firetruth* docked Bryssa went on station and held rallies. There were a few scuffles and arrests at each of them, but nobody tried to harm her again.

Strike spent the time in between her rallies talking to his contacts, and studying human political analyses. He said they often got it wildly wrong, but most 'opinion polls' as he called them were forecasting a win for Bryssa.

"Jorrak won't take defeat lightly," he said. "I'm noticing

there's more Collective Security at every rally Bryssa's holding. I'm following the investigation into her poisoning. Judiciary have started building a file against Jorrak for that, but they haven't proved a definite link between him and the dog project. They can't prove he was behind the poisoning attempt - yet."

The *Firetruth* continued her journey Centralward, and docked at Aadanna Station a day before *Thunderstrike*.

Strike had asked his Unit contacts to warn him if anyone noticed him following the *Firetruth*. So far, nobody had done so.

He didn't come to Aadanna often. The station was a key Central Spine location, the nearest one to Central Station and Earth. Strike didn't have Unit contacts in Station Security here, the risk of the Unit being discovered was too great. So he was nervous about Bryssa holding a rally here. He didn't have his usual level of data about it, and he didn't think he could risk sending his drones on station. He thought they'd be noticed by the extra security measures in force here now. So instead, Bahar and I were going to be his eyes at the rally.

We went on station two hours before it was due to start.

We met Chaye and Hyordis at a café a short walk away from the square where Bryssa was holding her rally. Chaye said the Employment Hub had been busy recently. It seemed that ship's crews who'd deserted the Outlier routes were now willing to work there again. Maybe Regulus's new CEO had a hand in that. Hyordis said they'd handled more shipments for the Outliers recently too.

This suspicious lion wondered if that was Jorrak trying to look good. He'd already denied he was abandoning the Outliers. Strike said most people didn't believe him any more.

"Do you know anything about Sister Strategy?" Bahar asked our contacts.

Both of them grinned. "Sure do. We're both members," Chaye said.

"Have you seen this woman with them?" Bahar sent over a recent image of Nyla.

"She's not part of the local team here," Hyordis replied. "Who is she?"

"We think this is Nyla Vatan. The last sister we're looking for. If you spot her, tell Strike, will you?"

By the time Bryssa's rally at Aadanna Station started the crowd filled the whole of the square. Bahar and I found a space on a first floor balcony of a tiered garden. It had a clear view of the back of the stage in the square below, and we hoped we'd be able to spot Nyla – if she turned up down there.

The rally was noisy, but we weren't focused on the crowd. We were looking for Nyla.

"There she is," Bahar said, and pointed her out to me.

Nyla was standing by the Sister Strategy banner, to the left of the stage, talking into a com. She wore a dark blue jacket that blended into the crowd. It didn't have anyone's logo on it.

The rally was noisy, with a lot of heckling. Part-way through Bryssa's speech I saw disturbances start at the edge of the crowd. They weren't aimed at Bryssa. This was people attacking her audience.

They're trying to start a riot, Strike said over our feed.

The crowd in the square became a whirling mass of people as the audience turned to attack their attackers. Soon it had become a full-blown riot.

Bahar and I tried to keep our attention on Nyla, but it

was hard with the crowd surging around the back of the stage, filling the space where she stood.

"Attention all citizens. If fighting does not cease within five minutes this square will be sealed and sleepgas deployed." The announcement from Station Security blared from nodes all around us, and it was very loud. It hurt my ears, and I snarled.

The riot started to break up. The hostiles had achieved their aim of disrupting Bryssa's speech, and nobody wanted to get sleepgassed.

"Where's Nyla?" Bahar asked. "I can't see her."

I searched for her too, but when the crowds thinned out behind the stage the spot where she'd stood was empty. The Sister Strategy banner had gone too.

Strike, can you see Nyla anywhere? Bahar asked.

Not on the public feeds. The whole Sister Strategy team seems to have disappeared.

So we've lost her again. I should've gone to ground level, gone in to talk to her there, Bahar said.

Too late for regrets, Strike replied. *The positives are that I guessed right and she did follow Bryssa Centralward. We'll pick up her trail again later.*

You hope, Bahar replied.

CHAPTER FOURTEEN

Strike recalled us to his shipbody right away. Station Security had started trawling files of the disturbance at Bryssa's rally. He didn't think they'd be interested in two people up on a first floor balcony, but we decided to leave anyway. The last thing we needed was to get held up here while Bryssa went on to Central.

The whole station was busy as we made our way back to *Thunderstrike*. Bahar led me to a lift lobby 20.2 minutes away from the square. She thought it might be quieter, but the lobby was full when we walked in. Most of the people had just exited the lifts, and many of them were in armour. I dropped back behind Bahar so that I didn't get my nose bruised, and she forced a path through to the lift cars for us.

Were those all Station Security? I asked over our feed.

I suspect so. I think we left just in time.

The car in front of us opened its doors. Six more armoured figures pushed their way past us. Bahar claimed the car and ushered me in, pushing the 'up' button before anyone could decide to join us.

We rode up two levels and across to the lobby nearest Strike's berth. This car had an irritating vibration in the floor, which bothered my paws. I kept lifting each one in turn to stop the uncomfortable tingling running through them. When it stopped and the doors opened I was glad to step out into the unmoving lobby.

The dock section near Strike's berth was busy too, and again I dropped back behind Bahar to avoid getting my nose bruised. Those idiots at the Predatorbot Programme never realised that our noses are sensitive as well as our whiskers. You could stop a Predatorbot with a heavy blow to its nose.

Bahar fought our way through to Strike's berth, and I relaxed as I walked up *Thunderstrike's* ramp. He opened the airlock door and let us in. "Come up to the rec area," he said. "We need to plan our next move."

Strike might not have had his drones on station, but he'd risked hacking into the station's own surveillance systems in an attempt to track Nyla. It hadn't worked. He still didn't know where she was.

Bahar got coffee and sprawled over a seat in the rec area. "So what now?" she asked.

"The *Collective's Firetruth* has asked for a line out

tomorrow. To Central Station."

"So Bryssa is going home," Bahar said.

"What did you expect? The election's getting close. She's probably planning on being on Earth for polling day."

He still called it that, although votes would continue to be received and counted from the Collective's vast sprawl of stations and worlds for at least seven days after.

"I suppose we need to go to Central then." Bahar didn't sound too enthusiastic about the idea.

"I don't want to go there. But I think I must." I knew Strike was nervous about putting himself into that web of tighter security, especially in the middle of an election campaign. "I've asked Chaye and Hyordis to brief me on what they know about things there. They confirm that security is tight, but they don't think I'll have any problems."

"You are a legitimate Starnavy ship," Bahar pointed out.

"A ship without any official orders. I think I need to get some before I arrive."

"How about tying us to the *Firetruth* somehow? Being a secret escort?" Bahar suggested.

"That's… yeah, maybe I could make that work. I need

to talk to our contacts about it."

We arranged our line out several hours behind the *Firetruth*, as usual. As Strike was undocking he got an update from Jamar. Jamar worked in Traffic Control at Central Station, and he was passing on a report of an attack on the station. Four ships had attacked Central without warning. Station's guns had destroyed them, but the incident meant the station was on high alert for traitors and other attacks. This was not what we needed.

Jamar told Strike that Starnavy IDs were being checked for every ship which downjumped at Central now. "That's a reminder to me and everyone else in the Unit to be extra careful," Strike said. "I'm sending out a bulletin on that to every member."

"How much damage did they do to the station?" Bahar asked.

"They managed to hole a small section of dock. Some casualties."

"So are we still going there?"

"We have to, if Nyla's there," I said. I couldn't abandon my mentor. I needed to see she was safe.

"I agree," Strike replied. "Jorrak's support is strongest on Central and Earth. He was Earth-born, and the locals support their own. The risk to Nyla will be at its greatest there. We have to follow her."

CHAPTER FIFTEEN

I didn't sleep well on our jump to Central Station. Bahar didn't either, and we were both yawning and tense as we approached our downjump.

Strike started wake-up of his troops while we were in transit. I wasn't sure if he wanted them awake to defend us, or whether he was expecting trouble on station. They were all awake an hour before we emerged into normal space. As Strike briefed them, Howin decided they should all get their armour on. That did nothing for my worries, especially when Strike told me and Bahar to get into our armour too.

"We don't know what we're facing there," he said. "If someone attacks us, I need to know you're safe."

"You think there's a chance of that?" I asked.

"Always a chance the wrong people will get hurt when a fight starts."

This was another way that Strike showed he cared for us. His core and memories would likely survive destruction of his shipbody. We'd only stand a chance of that if we were armoured. Strike knew that, and while he might tease us about being squishy meatbags, he was also aware of how vulnerable we were in the hostile nothingness of space.

I went to my quarters and let Strike's drones put my armour on. It had programmable camouflage, and could be unfolded in sections. When it only covered my back it passed for a fancy metallic coat for a petbot, especially when I'd programmed it to show a hideous pattern, or a 'naff logo', as Bahar called it.

The drones fastened the armour around my belly, and I extended the leg sections, lifting one paw at a time to let the armour seal under it. I kept my helmet retracted. I returned to the control room. Bahar had arrived before me. Strike counted us down to emergence, and as soon as we came into normal space he put the nav plot up on the wallscreen.

"The *Collective's Firetruth* has docked on the other side of station," he said. "On the Judiciary dock, so we won't get close to her. We'll have to rely on our contacts on station to pass on sightings of Nyla. I've already sent out that request, and a current image of her."

"I guess that's all we can do for now," Bahar said.

"It is." Strike sounded frustrated. Bahar often accused

him of being a 'control freak', but here he daren't be too visible. We couldn't afford for anyone to uncover the Unit, so Strike had to act like a legitimate Starnavy ship without any personal agenda. He always found that hard.

"Being asked for my ID again," he said. "I daren't refuse the request here."

There was a tense wait until he said, "ID's been accepted. We've got our line in. And it's a fast one."

"So far, so good," Bahar replied. "Let's hope it stays that way."

Nobody attacked us on the way in, and Strike docked safely four shipboard days later. As soon as he connected to the dock he said, "Local Commander's just contacted me. It's Commander Lazzhar, and he's a known Jorrak sympathiser. He wants you ashore for a debrief, Bahar. To discuss my recent missions."

Was that a touch of fear I heard in Strike's voice? I thought so.

"You think the Unit's been discovered?" Bahar asked.

"What else can it mean?"

"Maybe he doesn't like our focus on the Outliers. Or

maybe he wants us to brief him about them. Or… It could be half a dozen other things."

"I need to stop panicking, don't I?" Strike said.

"It never helps, in the end."

"I know. But I'm still anxious."

"I know you are. So where is this debrief?" Bahar asked.

Strike sent the room number and a route to the briefing room over to Bahar's implant. "Okay, I'm on it," she said, and left the control room.

She put on her captain's semi-dress uniform, and ten minutes later she was striding down *Thunderstrike's* ramp to the dock. I had to stay here, of course. I found that even harder when Strike sent our troops onto station, and it was only him and me left aboard.

"Now they're all gone I want you to help me review my logs," Strike said.

"You think people can discover the Unit through them?" I asked.

"That's what I need to check. I want to review my official logs for the last five Standards. Make sure I haven't added any references that don't sound Starnavy. I'm sending you the first batch. Check that they've all got proper Starnavy headers, Snap."

"Will do," I said.

As a Predatorbot, I have memories and processors implanted in my chest. I'm the home of last resort for Strike's core if someone tries to delete him. But it also means that I can handle his files.

I set searches going to find any message without Starnavy headers. Those returned a blank, so I ran the searches again, looking for keywords like 'Unit'. "I can't see anything suspect in that batch," I said.

"Good. Here's the second lot."

By the time Bahar reached the local Commander's office we'd worked back seven Standards, and Strike was as confident as he could be that his Starnavy files didn't reveal the Unit.

Of course, he had his shadow memories where key Unit data was stored. But only he and I knew they existed – and how to access them. To anyone else, that memory storage showed up as empty.

We finished the checks 5.3 minutes before Bahar entered the local Commander's office. For once, a busy station had worked in our favour. She'd had to wait 10.7 minutes to get a free lift car, and the extra delay had been welcome.

Strike had risked hacking into the security systems at the Commander's office complex. You'd think, with Central Station tightening its security, that the Starnavy would've updated its codes there too. But the ones Strike had gave him access to the system. He recorded the contact to one of his aliases, of course.

Commander Lazzhar was a hard-faced man with cropped silver hair and bright blue eyes. He also seemed to have a permanent frown. Bahar gave him a crisp salute, and sat down when ordered.

"I'm conducting a review of the missions our frigates have been on recently," he said. "It appears that *Thunderstrike* is being partisan."

Bahar managed to look surprised, and said, "I'm sorry, Sir. I don't follow."

"For the last year *Thunderstrike* has spent most of his time in the Outliers. More recently, Strike seems to have been following the *Collective's Firetruth* around. With one of the Presidential candidates aboard that ship, I can't help thinking you're providing unofficial support to her."

"We go where we're ordered. We've happened to be available at several ports when supplies have needed delivering, especially to the Outliers. It's my understanding that many Starnavy ships have been drafted in to do cargo runs there recently. This might be in response to the release of our President's confidential plan to abandon the Outliers." She was trying to deflect his attention away from our more recent missions. Surprisingly, it worked.

He glared at her, and she met and held his gaze with her neutral one. "Outlier Action were greatly upset by that report. Strike was in the right place to help the Outlier colonies, so of course he did. I can't see how that can be construed as being partisan. We well understand our duty to be impartial, especially during election campaigns." Bahar paused, and engaged the Commander with a fierce stare. "I can assure you that neither Strike nor I has used our Starnavy positions to advocate for any candidate in any election. We have kept our oath to 'serve all'."

The Commander didn't answer. He was flicking through files on his pad. *He's checking my logs*, Strike said. *Hope we did our job properly, Snap.*

CHAPTER SIXTEEN

After a too-long pause of 6.8 minutes the Commander spoke again. "I've reviewed Strike's files, and I can't see any anomalies there." He paused, and we read the unspoken phrase 'for now' in his voice.

"Is there anything else you want our help with, Sir?" Bahar asked.

The Commander fixed his gaze on her and held it there for 2.5 minutes. Bahar didn't flinch, or look away.

"For now, no," he said. "You're dismissed."

Bahar saluted sharply. "Thank you, Sir." She stood up and strode to the door before the Commander could think of some new challenge for her. She stepped out into the hallway, closed the door behind her, and let out a long breath. *That was close*, she said over our feed.

Too close, Strike replied.

So what now?

Stay there. Go meet our contacts on station.

Bahar met our on-station contacts Aeron and Jamar at the Fallingwater Tea Garden. Aeron was a machine intelligence working in Environmental, and her avatar took the form of a black-skinned professor. She wore a rich brocade robe decorated with gold embroidery, and carried a tablet in an ornate gilt frame. Jamar was a machine intelligence in Traffic Control. Her avatar was a unicorn with blue fur and a twisted horn.

The Tea Garden was in the middle of one of Central Station's biggest parks. Huge rock walls surrounded the café's terrace on three sides, and in the middle of them a high waterfall tumbled down to a clear pool beneath. A sound shield reduced the noise from the waterfall, so that people sitting at the tables could hear each other talk.

"So how's things?" Bahar asked when she'd ordered her coffee.

"Tense," Aeron said. "I've lost count of how many emergency drills we've done. Somebody's expecting trouble here."

"We have heard that local Commanders are cracking down on expressions of support by Starnavy personnel for any Presidential candidate," Jamar said.

That's close to denying Starnavy personnel the right to freedom of political choice, Strike replied. *I wonder if Jorrak has a finger in that pie. I'm sending my troops off to talk to some people about that.*

Be careful, Aeron replied. *Jorrak's becoming increasingly desperate – and ruthless.*

When Bahar's meeting with our contacts ended Strike recalled her to his shipbody. He seemed anxious, and risked hacking into the dock's vid system to track her progress.

Nobody attacked her, and she appeared in Strike's rec area 9.3 minutes later. Strike had started production of her favourite blend of coffee as soon as she came through his lockout gate, and the steaming mug was ready the moment she stepped into the rec area. Strike teased her about her coffee addiction, but he also fed it.

"Do you think that Commander suspects the Unit exists?" she asked as she sipped her coffee.

"I don't think so. Commander Lazzhar is a Jorrak fan. I suspect he's recruiting people for Jorrak's personal hit squad."

"Was he trying to recruit us?" Bahar sounded shocked at the idea.

"I think it was the first overture."

I had no idea what one of those was, but the thought

that someone was trying to recruit us to keep Jorrak in power was worrying. Would this Commander be tracking our movements now?

"I've been searching Starnavy databases, looking for evidence that Jorrak's giving partisan orders to Starnavy local Commanders. Our contacts have turned up some odd orders, but they don't directly benefit Jorrak. At this stage, I can't prove he's corrupting the Starnavy's ideals."

I knew Strike desperately wanted to ensure that Jorrak got voted out at the election, but he wasn't going to interfere in it. For one reason, it would get him uninstalled fast if a human discovered he'd been trying to influence the results.

Humans had been living alongside sapient machine intelligences for over a century now, but there were still traces of 'AIs are taking over the universe' mentality among some societies. Those were the ones living on planets. Anybody who set foot on a station knew they only survived there because machine intelligences kept them safe. Even so, Strike had to be careful.

"We need to focus on finding Nyla," Bahar said.

"Got some information which I think is about her,"

Strike said. "Someone passed Aeron an image and name. I'm 98% certain the person is Nyla. She goes by the name Saria Wbubu these days."

"Why choose that name?" Bahar was sensitive to people appropriating other's cultures. Strike had told me her ancestors had suffered badly from that.

"It's a cipher, based on Vatan. And too easy to crack."

"If you're looking for it," Bahar pointed out.

"Yes, okay. Maybe I am fretting too much. I do think it's time we tried to make contact with her though."

"Will she want to meet us?"

"You'll have to go to Bryssa's rally here later and find out."

I went on station with Bahar to observe Bryssa's rally. She'd taken over Central Station's biggest park, and it was crammed full of people.

"Now we'll see how much support she has closer to home," Strike said.

We worked our way around to the back of the stage. Bahar wanted to be at ground level this time, ready to intercept Nyla when the meeting was over. We weren't going to get stuck on some first floor balcony this time. There weren't any surrounding this park, but you know what I mean.

The rally was noisy, and Bryssa got heckled a lot. I could see Bahar looking more anxious as the meeting went on.

Then fighting broke out around the stage. *Sending Howin in*, Strike said over our feed. Bahar moved forward too, but a squad of armoured people pushed in front of her. In seconds the space at the back of the stage was full of people. I saw them pushing and shoving each other, and the banners of Sister Strategy and False Manifesto were torn down.

Can't reach Nyla, Howin said over our feed. *Somebody's formed a cordon around her.*

Bahar swore, and pushed forward again, but someone shoved her roughly away.

Got vid now, Strike said. *I think this might be a Jorrak squad. I've found Nyla on the vid. They're arresting her. I need to track her progress. Arrow's sending me a feed. Yeah, Nyla's been grabbed. Trying to check if they're Security logos. No they aren't. Howin, here's the co-*

ordinates.

Moving to intercept, Howin confirmed.

The fighting behind the stage had stopped, and Bryssa decided to wrap up her speech. We didn't stay to listen. We were already on the move. We had to intercept that rogue snatch squad before they took Nyla somewhere and harmed her. Strike had sent Bahar and me to an alternative hallway, in case the squad changed its direction. Howin and the troops were already gone from the square.

My heart thundered as I trotted along beside Bahar. Nyla was in danger. And we'd totally failed to keep her safe .

CHAPTER SEVENTEEN

Got her location, Strike said 10.2 minutes later. *They're going to Detention Block 2-Q-12 on this level. Bahar, you're nearest. Howin, get over there.*

Going, Bahar said, and turned down a cross-corridor. Strike had sent me the location plot too. We were only a few minutes away from Nyla. I trotted along beside Bahar. She wore light armour under her jacket, and I had my armour on but retracted. We couldn't afford to get into a serious firefight, and I worried about how we'd retrieve Nyla.

Coming up on your position, Howin said. *Keep out of the firing line.*

Hurry, then. They're about to take her inside, Bahar replied.

A flurry of movement around the curve of the hallway resolved into Howin and the troops. They slid into place between the snatch squad and the detention block. I kept my attention on the figure they were herding along. It was definitely Nyla. I recognised her scent. She was shouting that she'd been kidnapped and yelling for help. Soon her captors would hit her to shut her up.

"Release her!" Howin roared. "Who ordered you to snatch this woman?"

"Who in hell are you? We got orders to arrest her," the snatch squad leader growled.

Howin stood her ground, and the pistol was suddenly in her hand. The troops followed her lead, and now there were twenty armed people facing the snatch squad. I kept out of the firing line, but I was fretting. Nyla was right here, and I couldn't rescue her, and she might get hurt…

Through my panic I heard Howin say, "Who gave you your orders?"

"None 'o yer business." The thug pointed his pistol at Howin's chest.

She returned the gesture, and saw him blink in surprise. "We've heard rumours of bent elements in Station Security. People bribed by our President to remove inconvenient people. So I gotta ask you – what's she charged with?"

"None 'o yer business." A different tough tried his luck at intimidating Howin. This time Rance stepped up and pointed his pistol back at the man.

"Every citizen's business to see law's fairly administered. You arrest someone, they gotta know why.

So why did you arrest her?" Rance demanded.

"Chief of Security here ordered it."

"And why would that be?" Howin wasn't letting him get away with that. "She was part of a peaceful rally. Can't see she did anything illegal. So what's she going to be charged with?"

"I dunno. Haven't charged her with anythin'."

"If you haven't charged her with anythin', then you gotta let her go," Rance insisted. "See, if she goes into detention, we're releasing the vid on the newsnets. People here are claiming the Security Chief's been bought by Jorrak, to silence opposition to him. This detention looks pretty much like one 'o those."

The first thug cocked his head, as if listening to something on his feed. Howin tensed, and checked her pistol. Rance checked his too. Were the thugs going to get an order to attack? Nyla was still in the middle of this confrontation, and I didn't think she was wearing armour. She could get badly hurt here.

CHAPTER EIGHTEEN

After 6.3 tense minutes the thugs lowered their weapons. "Chief's cancelled the order," the lead one said. "Take her."

Howin and the troops moved in around Nyla, and got her away from the thugs. Bahar approached her and said, "We need to talk. Please come with us."

"Who the hell are you to dictate what I do? Damned corrupt Starnavy!"

Nyla's unexpected response made Bahar blink. "We've just saved you from corrupt Starnavy," she said. "Those thugs weren't official. And I'm Bahar Zivai. I'm the Captain of *Thunderstrike*."

"Strike? Oh." Nyla looked down at me.

"This is PB-30-12," Bahar said. The hardness on Nyla's face melted away.

"My name is Snap now," I said. My throat felt choked. The sight of my mentor had made me feel... emotional, as Bahar would describe it.

"We need to get off this station for your safety," Bahar said. "Strike is tasked with keeping all your sisters safe. We'll tell you about them if you come aboard."

"So you can kidnap me instead?"

"No. So that we can discuss you and your sisters somewhere secure."

"We've spent the last two Standards looking for you all," I said. "We're keeping them safe." A massive stab of disappointment had flooded my body at Nyla's hostile words. I'd imagined us just walking up to her and… saving her. Bahar says that I can be very naïve at times. I think this is one of them.

"We know you're working with Sister Strategy," Bahar said. "The trouble is, Jorrak does too. I'm sure he ordered those thugs to snatch you. I don't think you'll ever be safe campaigning here. You're too close to Jorrak's power base."

Nyla sighed, and the fight went out of her. "Rayye said so. I didn't want to listen. We're getting to the crucial part of Bryssa's campaign. I can't walk away from it now."

"You don't have to do that. Just campaign somewhere safer. And I know Strike's keen to meet you again."

Nyla shook her body, as if throwing off her tension. "I know you're right about the dangers," she said. "Okay, take me to *Thunderstrike*."

The station was very busy now, and Bahar called Howin and the troops in and put Nyla in the middle of them. That worked while we walked down the wide hallways, but the squad had to spread out for some of the smaller ones.

I was anxious as we made our way along them. My anxiety flared into deeper worry as we came out onto Strike's dock. We were only two berths away from *Thunderstrike*, but the dock was crammed with people.

The squad was forced to separate. I couldn't see anything other than a press of uniformed bodies around me. Several bumped into my nose. It was getting sore, and I was finding it hard to control my reactions. I couldn't bite those people, but I wanted to.

Our progress along the dock was slow. Just before we reached *Thunderstrike's* berth someone barged into Howin. She didn't often stumble, but this man was taller and broader than her.

Rance, get him, Howin said on our feed.

Rance was ahead of me, and pulled his pistol from his pocket and flicked it on. As the big man made a grab for Nyla's arm, Rance stunned him. He pushed the falling body away from Nyla, and the troops closed up around her again.

Get aboard. Fast, Strike said over our feed.

Howin hustled Nyla towards *Thunderstrike's* lockout gate, and Strike opened it as they approached. Howin swept Nyla up the ramp and didn't slow her pace until she was safely in the airlock. I was at the back of the group now, and I didn't want to get snatched again either.

One of the rogue squad stepped in front of me, but I wasn't stopping. I turned my shoulder to him, and used my lion's strength to push him out of the way.

Hurry, Snap, Strike said. *Another one's coming for you.*

I reached the lockout gate as somebody else grabbed my tail. That I won't tolerate. I was about to turn and snarl at my attacker when Howin said, *Snap, keep your head down.* An energy burst sizzled above my back, and I heard a cry and a thump from behind me. The grip on my tail loosened.

Come on, Snap, Strike said, and I trotted up the ramp. As soon as I came into the airlock Strike closed it behind me.

"Welcome aboard *Thunderstrike*, Nyla." Strike was into his charming introductions bit, as he called it. "That wasn't quite the welcome I had planned."

"I seem to be running into things like that regularly now," she said.

"Let's take you up to the rec area, then we can talk," Bahar replied, steering Nyla into the lift car.

I let them go first. I rode up in the lift alone, and Strike let me into the control room. "How are you feeling, Snap?" he asked.

"Strange," I replied. "We've spent so long searching for Nyla, and now we've found her I don't know what to say to her. She's changed."

"So have you," Strike pointed out. "You've both been to other places, done other things since you left the Programme. You have to talk to her, Snap."

"What if she doesn't… care about me any more?"

"What if she's sitting there thinking the same about you?"

"That's… You think she is?"

"You won't know how either of you are feeling unless you talk to each other. So be a big, brave, Predatorbot, and go talk to your mentor."

My heart was thudding hard as I walked into the rec area. Nyla looked round as I came in, and smiled at me. "It's so good to see you again," she said. "So you're called Snap now? I'm glad you've got a name."

"Strike gave it to me. He wouldn't let me keep my Programme label."

"Good. Labelling sapient beings by numbers is just wrong. Monsters!"

"We've shut down several offshoots of the Programme on our travels," Bahar said. "I can't tell you too much about what we do, but where we can, we challenge Jorrak's evil and corruption."

"Good," Nyla replied. "That's what Sister Strategy are doing."

"We think Jorrak's got himself a rogue Starnavy squad. People who are loyal to him personally," Strike said. "Those thugs who tried to kidnap you wore Starnavy uniforms, but they had no identifiers on them. My considered opinion is that if you go back out there and start campaigning again, they'll try to snatch you again."

"I need to keep the pressure up on Jorrak. I'm running liaison between Sister Strategy and Bryssa Meir's campaign team. We all want Bryssa as President. But you're telling me I need to give that up. I can't. The stakes are too high."

"We have a suggestion for you," Bahar said. "How do you feel about re-establishing contact with your sisters?"

Nyla shrugged. "They won't talk to me. They cut me off. We argued."

"What if I told you they were keen to re-establish contact?"

Nyla stared at Bahar, and I saw the flare of hope in Nyla's eyes. "I'd love that," she said. "I've really, really, missed them."

"Then it's time to make a decision," Strike said. "I've received a tip-off that Jorrak is trying to order a lockdown of this station. I don't know if that's about you, but I don't plan on getting stuck here. The local Commander's refusing to carry out the order at present. I want to be out of here before she makes her mind up."

"Are we ready to go?" Bahar asked.

"You know me better than that. I'm fuelled up, printer stocks replenished, provisional line out granted, thanks to Jamar. So, Nyla, do I take you to see your sisters?"

She sighed, then gave a little laugh. "Here's me trying to

convince myself that nobody else can run a campaign. Sheer arrogance. Someone else can pick it up now. I'll leave, but I need to talk to people at Sister Strategy first."

"You have half an hour to reach them," Strike said. "Then I'm leaving."

Nyla contacted three people, two in Sister Strategy, one on Bryssa's campaign team. Bahar and I left her alone in the rec area to talk to them in private. The troops were mooching around in the galley and the quarters they shared while she talked. When Bahar and I went to check on her half an hour later, Nyla seemed a little subdued. She said she'd spoken to the people she needed to reach, and she'd told them she was leaving.

"Good," Strike said. "I have a fast line out, and we're going fast. Get to the control room, Bahar, Snap. I need your eyes on the nav plot."

"We're coming," Bahar replied.

Nyla reached out a hand to me, and I walked towards her. She stroked my head, her hand warm on my fur. "I'm so glad you're thriving, Snap," she said. "We must have a long talk later."

"We will," I promised.

As I padded down the hallway behind Bahar my emotions did that thing she called her 'spirits soaring'. What a strange expression. Emotions can't fly. But now, with this joyous feeling making my heart flutter, I finally understood what that meant.

Strike had the nav plot up on the wallscreen when we arrived in the control room. "Did you really need our help with this?" I asked as I settled into my space beside Bahar's seat.

"More like support for my fretting," he admitted.

"What? The great Strike is worried?" Bahar teased.

"I am. And yes, I need you to spot anything coming close to us. I'm going so fast I need to keep my focus on my line."

That's when I knew Strike really was anxious. "You think we might not make it out in time?" I asked.

"I need to be able to say I didn't get any lockdown order, and Jamar's just told me Commander Lazzhar's gone to a meeting with the Traffic Control Chief."

"To discuss the lockdown," Bahar said.

"That's my reading of it. I need to be ready to jump

before that order gets to me. And that's going to be close timing."

It was a tense journey out to our jump point. Bahar and I spotted two potential problems, both civilian ships which looked like they might cross our line. Strike warned both of them off, and the first one changed course fast. The second one was a little more reluctant, until Strike reminded the captain that he was a Starnavy frigate and well able to blast any obstructions out of his way.

Eventually the captain changed course, but Strike had his shields up as he passed by the ship. He wasn't convinced that it wasn't a raider. We'd tangled with several of those in the last few Standards.

We passed the ship without shots being fired, but Strike kept on at full speed beyond it. The nearer we got to the jump point, the more tense he became. "Jumping in five minutes," he warned.

Strike counted us down to insertion. At the ten-second mark a coms line on the console flashed. Strike ignored it, and continued with his countdown.

Once we'd cleared transition he opened the message.

"Lockdown order," he said. "That idiot Commander's gone and done it. Deleting message from coms logs now. Hope we don't run into trouble on downjump."

CHAPTER NINETEEN

Strike was tense as we approached our downjump at Aadanna Station. He and Bahar had had a discussion – more of an argument really – about whether we'd be in danger there. Bahar thought he was over-reacting. We'd been so close to jump that nobody would know whether he'd received the lockdown order or not.

"The coms buoys will have a record of sending it, with probable receipt time," Strike pointed out.

"Probable." Bahar stressed the word. "No receipt confirmation means its calculation was wrong. Okay?"

"Okay," Strike said reluctantly.

Sometimes I wanted to grab idiot humans and sit them down to listen to the conversations of the sapient machine intelligences they'd created. Show them how messed-up their idea of heartless killing machines was. And how badly they'd failed there. I was hoping we'd be able to do that for the Predatorbot Programme after the election. Provided the right President got elected, of course.

Strike counted us down to emergence, and I had to confess that his nervousness was affecting me too. What if the Commander had sent on a request to arrest Strike here?

As we emerged into black and stars I told myself not to be stupid. Nobody would worry that one frigate had escaped the lockdown order.

Unless that person knew about the Unit.

Thunderstrike, line in coming over to you now." The first voice we heard from Aadanna Station was a Traffic Controller's, and it was calm. No threatening to arrest us, just business as usual.

Beside me, Bahar let out a long breath, and flopped back into her seat. "We made it," she said.

"We did," Strike replied, "and Hyordis just contacted me. Things are busy here, but no trouble. We've got a slow line in, though, so I can catch up on the news before we dock. I'm requesting a fast turnaround. My feeling is that we should get Nyla away from the Central Worlds fast."

"You think Jorrak's still looking for her there?" I asked.

"I think he'll be looking for her right up to election day. Ah, got the fast turnaround approved. Looks like nobody's going to arrest us here."

119

Our departure was the fastest Strike had ever managed. He'd sent in his resupply list ahead of docking, and supplies started to arrive at his lock 5.8 minutes after we docked. That was impressive.

His refuel was almost as fast, and 12.4 hours after we arrived Strike left his dock and headed out into the deep black again.

We were bound for Ataret Station. As we made our way out to the jump point Strike received a file from Jamar. "Jamar says the Central Station Commander is questioning the lockdown order. He's reluctant to implement it, and as of now, ships are still going into jump. The Chief apparently asked for a confirmation from Starnavy HQ that the order is genuine."

"Which should expose Jorrak's rogue actions if it isn't," Bahar said.

"Indeed." There was satisfaction in Strike's tone. "And we're going into jump in five minutes."

No more orders came in before we jumped, and once we were in transition Strike relaxed.

Bahar yawned, and said, "It's far too long since I slept."

"It's far too long since both of you slept," Strike said in

that indulgent voice he often used with us. Some days it annoyed Bahar, and she'd say, 'Stop it, Strike. I'm not your child.' I like him fussing over me.

He let me into my quarters, and told me Nyla had already gone to sleep. I still hadn't had that long talk with her, and I was determined to have it when I woke up.

I slept for 9.7 hours, and Strike fed me in my quarters. He said Nyla was in the rec area, and now would be a good time to talk to her.

My nervousness returned as I entered the room. Nyla was sprawled in a seat, her attention on a pad. She put it down and smiled at me when I walked in.

"Hello, Snap," she said, and held out a hand to me. I padded over to her, and sat down by her side. She ran her fingers through my fur, like she had when I was a little cub, then stopped. "I shouldn't do that, should I? You're not a cub needing reassurance now. You're a big, strong lion."

"I still worry about things," I said. "They thought they were creating heartless killing machines. Predatorbots are the opposite."

"Good. I'd hoped you'd grow up like that. It was what I

was trying to trigger in you all." She sighed. "I had so many arguments with the Programme's staff about you. I should've left earlier, not had anything to do with it. But they bribed me with money, and made it hard for me to get another job."

That's another way humans are weird. Their biggest religion is the worship of money. Some of them have so much credit that they could never spend it all if they lived to be three hundred Standards old.

"I'm sorry, Snap."

"For what? You always cared for us," I said.

"Yes, I did. Sometimes you needed a hug or a stroke. You'd never known a mother's care. I tried to give that to you. Especially you, Snap. You were always the one I bonded with best, the one who was least like the killing machines they wanted."

"I am. Unlike humans."

"Not all humans kill, Snap. I've never killed anyone."

"I'm glad."

She reached down a hand and stroked my head. I pushed my body into her leg. She kissed the top of my head and said, "I love you, Snap. I always did."

My heart gave an irregular thump, and I raised my head to her. "I've missed you. We've been looking for you for Standards. I was so afraid Jorrak's thugs might've killed you…"

"I tried to ignore them at first, until I got hurt. I didn't want to leave the campaign, but now I realise I must. Jorrak has turned beyond nasty, and we need to get rid of him – for all our sakes."

CHAPTER TWENTY

Strike's anxiety grew again as we approached our downjump at Ataret Station. We were getting close to Davion, the planetary safe haven Strike had helped to create for the Vatan sisters.

I tried not to notice the checks he did on his shields and weapons systems. That was what he always did when he suspected there'd be trouble on downjump. Bahar said it was the equivalent of a human checking that all the doors in their apartment were locked before they went to bed. It was a reassurance, a way he told himself he was safe.

We didn't know if we'd be safe here. Strike had received that lockdown order before jump, and if he hadn't been as clever as he thought he was at fooling the coms system we'd be in trouble here.

Both I and Bahar were in the control room for emergence, of course. But we weren't going to admit to Strike that we were nervous too.

"Downjump in three… two… one…" he announced.

We emerged into normal space, and Strike acquired the nav plot. "Very busy here. A lot of civilian ships."

"I wonder if they're Outlier Action getting organised,"

Bahar said.

It took seven shipboard days for *Thunderstrike* to get into dock. As we approached it Traffic Control sent an emergency course change to Strike.

"Some idiot civilian's skimming close to station," he said. "Not answering hails to change course."

"Are we expecting an attack?" Bahar asked.

"It's sloppily planned if it is. Station's short-range guns are on them."

"Oh. Right."

Not every station had short-range weapons. Most tried to blast problems out of existence before they got close enough to cause the kind of havoc these civilians were doing now.

"Why didn't Traffic Control stop them further out?" I asked.

"Because Station Security were ordered not to interfere. By their Chief. Who is now in custody, and the Deputy's taken over operations."

"Rogue Security on station?" I asked. That hadn't happened before, but I don't know why I hadn't thought of the possibility. Quietly taking over stations from the inside and letting their forces dock would be a clever move. Was this Jorrak, or Outlier Action? I really didn't like the idea of being caught between the two of them.

Station Security dealt with the idiot civilian. They sent out a magnetic capture tug, and grabbed the ship's hull with its powerful magnets. Strike said that was a rough way to get captured, and the magnets fried your ship's systems. He said the idiots deserved having their ship trashed. He still couldn't figure out what they'd been up to out there.

With the threat removed, station returned to normal operation, and we got into dock safely. By then Strike had made contact with our Unit people here, and we already knew the current situation on Ataret.

A dozen Outlier Action ships had been impounded, and were currently in the shipyard having key components of their drives removed. "There are arrest warrants out for their captains on Olianna and Dracen Stations," Strike said. "This is Station Security's way of ensuring they don't slip from custody."

"Unless they're Jorrak's people. He'll have some way to

get them out," I said.

"Maybe that's behind this move too. The Deputy Commander is very keen to root out other rogues. Judiciary have the Chief in custody still. So far, they've not been able to make any connections to Jorrak through him."

"Disappointing," Bahar said. "I'm sure there are some. Can we go on-station here safely?"

"Yes, and I need you to meet our contacts before we leave for Davion."

He didn't say why. He didn't need to. We needed as much data as we could get, and Strike didn't trust the coms systems here to be secure. So we had to do this the old way, talking face-to-face, as Bahar called it. I know Strike would never forgive himself if he took Nyla to Davion and the sisters got hurt.

And neither would I.

Bahar and I met Tyger, Raptan, and Nuru in a swanky new café overlooking Nikkita Park. The place was all plas and bright metal, and my claws clicked on the plaswood floor as I walked in.

Our contacts were a diverse bunch. The blue and silver

iridescent stripes of Tyger's avatar glittered in the harsh lights of the café. Raptan's silver eagle avatar had a touch of iridescence to it also. Next to all that sparkle, Nuru's black skin looked even darker. As a human appearing in her real form, she seemed like the odd one out.

They settled at a table and Bahar and Nuru ordered food. When it had arrived Nuru took out a shield cylinder and activated it, cutting us off from the noise outside.

"So how's things?" Bahar asked.

Nuru spoke up. She was what Strike called a 'political analyst'. He said it was a fancy name for people who guessed the outcome of elections. "Most of the analysts think Bryssa has a real chance of winning now," she said. "There was a hustings on Central Station two days ago. Both Jorrak and Bryssa were there. Jorrak made sexist remarks about Bryssa."

"How did she reply?" Bahar asked.

"She called him out on it. But it was Sister Strategy who went crazy. They rage-posted all over the newsnets about him, claiming that he'd limit women's rights if he won the election. They're urging every woman to vote against him for their own safety."

"That doesn't always work," Bahar replied.

She was referring to an extraordinary period in Earth's old history. The women of one of the major powers had helped to elect a convicted criminal who was a rapist. She'd never been able to work out why women had voted against their own interests. Even from this far in the future, it still made Bahar furiously angry.

"We've heard rumours that Jorrak's seriously worried about losing. And the darker rumours are that he'll do anything to cling onto power," Tyger said.

"Is that normal election talk, or something deeper?" Bahar asked.

"Something deeper. A lot of people are worried about what he's planning to do next."

We spent 2.7 hours with our contacts at the café. Bahar and Nuru talked election-speak. Tyger said there'd been a larger number of Starnavy ships than usual going Centralward.

Raptan agreed with the analysis. The silver eagle avatar clicked its beak in annoyance. "We even had ships standing off station waiting for berths one day. Then when they all dock they're requesting fast turnarounds. We haven't been able to cope with those on two days. The Starnavy's pushing station to its limits."

"The official Starnavy, or Jorrak's private troops?" Bahar asked.

Raptan clicked the avatar's beak again. "Now that is the question, ain't it?" The avatar cocked its head, indicating a feed message. "Being recalled to duty," she said. "Gonna have to break up this meeting."

Bahar stood up. "I think we should be going too," she said. "Thanks for the updates, folks."

As we walked onto the dock where Strike was berthed he contacted us. *Think you should hurry back to me*, he said over our feed.

Why? Bahar asked.

Tyger's just told me forty Starnavy ships have docked here in the last day. That's more than they've ever seen in one group. They're going Centralward, and they're on 'election duties'.

Who for? Bahar asked.

Exactly. I don't want to get drafted into Jorrak's defence squad, so hurry on back.

We're hurrying, Bahar replied, and increased her stride.

She didn't run. Running figures always attracted the attention of dock security systems, and probably got vid of you forwarded to a machine intelligence for review. We didn't want to draw attention to ourselves, so Bahar strode out in that 'I'm busy and on a mission' stride humans everywhere used.

I could smell her scent turning anxious as we got close to *Thunderstrike's* berth. We reached it, and Strike opened the lockout gate and let us aboard. Bahar's anxious scent dissipated.

We rode up in the lift and went to the rec area. "So what have we got?" Bahar asked as she dropped into a seat there.

"A lot of Starnavy activity, going both ways," Strike replied. "Raptan's been trying to track the traffic flows. There seems to be a general recall Centralwards, but a counter group are going to the Outliers. She hasn't yet worked out whether both groups have legitimate orders."

"You think one might be Jorrak's troops?"

"I do. Oh, now we've got something. There's a squad been assigned to go to Davion."

"Why?" Bahar's anxious scent had returned.

"To 'put down a rebellion'," Strike replied.

"What rebellion? What's happened there?" Now I was worried too.

"Nothing, according to the updates I got from our contacts there an hour ago."

"Jorrak's found the Vatan sisters," I said.

CHAPTER TWENTY ONE

"Raptan's getting us a priority line out," Strike said. "We need to be on the move a.s.a.p. Before Jorrak's hit squad departs."

"We sure do," Bahar agreed.

"Raptan's queried the legitimacy of that order with the Chief. It came to Traffic Control with no official Starnavy headers or codes on it."

"Here we go again," I said.

"Yes. Fortunately, the Traffic Control Chief shares Raptan's unease, and is refusing to action the order until he receives official confirmation that it's legitimate. Which, so far, hasn't arrived."

"They'll just forge the orders," Bahar said.

"Agreed," Strike replied. "But I can't defend Davion alone. I need help."

My body had gone all shivery. We'd put three of the Vatan sisters down there, onto a planet Strike had assured us was a safe haven. And now it wasn't safe, and…

Breathe, Snap. Panicking never helps. You really should've learned that by now.

"We've got thirty Unit ships here. I need to set up a

conference with them fast, explain why it's important they accept my bogus orders to go to Davion. I'm already securing coms lines for it. We're doing this over a vid link."

The Unit conference took place half an hour later. Bahar and I went to the rec room to talk to the ships. Nyla hadn't been invited. She was busy in her quarters, studying a huge download of political updates Strike had got for her.

Strike had extended one long wall of the rec room to show the avatars and captains of all thirty ships. Their images were on the screen when we walked in. That… was rather intimidating.

"I'll keep this brief," Strike said. "A task force is being mustered to 'put down a rebellion' on Davion. There is no rebellion on Davion. It's very important that mission doesn't succeed. There are some VIPs on Davion who need protecting. I'm not sharing the details here for security reasons.

"Jorrak is sending troops down to the planet, and I need the Unit's ships to send down their own troops to oppose them."

"You're sure they're Jorrak's thugs?" Arrow asked.

"I am."

"Why does he want to harm people on Davion?"

"Because they've opposed his campaign. And because some of them know inconvenient truths and are campaigning against him."

"So how do we do this?" Honour asked.

"By being willing to depart as soon as Raptan can schedule your line out. I won't give you muster co-ordinates for Davion. We might find some of Jorrak's ships already there. And… I've just got my line out. Is everybody bought into the op?"

One by one the ships and their captains agreed to join the task force. "Good," Strike said. "I'm wrapping this up. "We'll talk again when we're all at Davion."

Strike left his dock an hour later. By then Raptan had scheduled outbound lines for all thirty of the Unit's ships.

Our troops were milling around the rec area, eating, and querying various bits of information with Strike. Howin and Rance were discussing tactics with him. I knew Strike was still worried about his decision to bring a Unit task force here. Howin often acted as his 'sounding-board', as Bahar put it, somebody who examined his plans – and wasn't afraid to tell him if she thought he'd got it wrong.

This time she endorsed his plan, and Bahar and I went to the galley to meet Nyla and let her know what was happening. Most of the Unit ship departures would be during station's 'night'. Hopefully that meant there'd be less people about to notice that a sizeable number of them were leaving almost together.

Strike was anxious as he made his way out to the jump point. If the task force going out to Davion turned out to be an official Starnavy squad, we could find ourselves in trouble there.

"Tyger's just sent me a file," he said. "Jorrak's contacted Ataret Traffic Control, demanding the Chief issues the line outs for his ships. He's threatening to get the Chief dismissed if she doesn't action the orders to schedule the squad's departure immediately.

"Unfortunately, she's agreed to do so. But the first ship departure isn't going to be for another twelve hours. We've taken up all the earlier slots."

"So we'll get to Davion before they do?" I asked.

"We will," Strike said. "And we're going to need every minute of that advantage."

CHAPTER TWENTY TWO

We downjumped at Davion and Strike immediately sent communications to our Unit contacts down there. The troops took over the rec area again for a last-minute planning session with our contacts on planet.

Bahar, Nyla, and I kept out of their way. We sat in the galley, and the humans drunk endless cups of coffee. Strike contacted Fia, and the vid showed Rhian and Merrill sitting in the room with her. Fia squinted at the screen. "Nyla? Is that you?"

"It is." Nyla's voice had a wobble to it.

"Thank God! We've been so worried about you. It was a very dark time after we…"

"It was for me too," Nyla said, cutting her off. "I've had to lie low. Jorrak's thugs were hunting me. I…"

"We need to plan for now," Bahar said. "Sorry to cut short your reunion, but a task force is being despatched here to 'put down a rebellion'."

"What? There's no…" Fia's face went hard. "That bastard Jorrak's found us, hasn't he?"

"We believe so," Strike said. "I've organised a force of ships to oppose him, but I don't think we'll be able to stop his troops landing there."

"What do we do? This house is so isolated. We have nowhere to hide here."

"You're going to have to leave home, I'm afraid," Bahar said. "Go into hiding in a secure place."

"Where? This a wildworld. We don't…"

"You do have places," Strike said. "You just don't know about them. I've been liaising with my contacts down there for the last half Standard. They've built a good network of places to go. I don't want to say too much about them, but you will need to leave your house.

"Pack the essentials. Changes of clothing, any tech you need. And be ready to leave when my troops arrive." Strike sent images of our squad leaders to them. "These are Howin and Rance. They're my team leaders. They'll come to your house and get you to safety. Be sure you're ready to go as soon as they arrive."

As Strike cut the line I said, "I want to go down with them."

Strike hesitated, then said, "It might be dangerous."

"I'm a big, brave, Predatorbot."

He laughed. "Trapped by my own words! Okay. But

be careful, Snap."

I walked to my quarters, and Strike's drones put my armour on. Then I went down to Deck Four. As the lift descended I thought that Strike never fretted about his troops going into danger the way he worried about me. True, they were trained for it and I wasn't. Nyla had snatched me away from the Programme before my combat training started.

I stepped into the vehicle bay and the deck chilled my paws as usual. I trotted towards the Xenophon's ramp and set my paws on it as the last trooper went through the airlock. Howin peered out and said, "Hurry up, Snap."

There was no tone of censure in her voice. Instead, I thought I heard satisfaction. I came into the airlock and Strike closed the door behind me. I walked through into the passenger compartment and found a space to sit by the equipment lockers, out of the reach of the troops' boots.

"Going out now," Strike announced.

I couldn't see anything from where I sat, but it was dark on Fia's part of Davion right now anyway. There were few buildings down there, and not much would show up even if I could look through a viewport.

"Dropping now," Strike said.

The whine of the shuttle's powerplant changed tone, then we were diving. I had to dig my claws into the deck to stay upright. Now I was glad I couldn't see out. I'd done many shuttle drops, but the sight of those fierce flames bouncing off the shuttle's shields still scared me every time.

"Re-entry complete," Strike announced. "Bringing you up to Fia's house now."

Strike landed the shuttle as lightly as usual, and Howin stood up. I went to the airlock with her. She looked down at me and nodded, but said nothing.

Strike let us out and I padded beside Howin over the crisp, cold grass towards the veranda which wrapped around Fia's house. My paws were soon chilled. Howin's boots thudded on the wooden steps as she climbed them to the front door. I came up beside her as she rapped on the door in the code we'd agreed with the sisters. I heard bolts being slid back, and the click of a lock. The door opened a crack.

"It's Howin and Snap," Howin said.

The door opened wider, and I could see shadowy figures behind it. The lights in the house were off.

"We need to move," Howin said.

"We're coming." That was Fia's voice. She led the three of them out, slinging a heavy pack over her shoulder as she came outside. Rhian and Merrill followed her, each with their own pack. Fia turned to lock the door, then said, "No point in securing the place. It might not be here when we come back."

"We'll try to see that it is," Howin replied, and hustled the sisters over to the shuttle.

When we were all inside Fia asked, "Where are you taking us?"

"To a secure bunker in the mountains."

"We don't have bunkers."

"You didn't until half a Standard ago," Howin replied. "Some people have been very busy recently building you some defences."

"Oh. It's us they're after, isn't it?" Merrill asked.

"The task force someone is sending here isn't official Starnavy. Strike didn't want you getting hurt if we have to deal with them." Howin didn't exactly say yes, but she hadn't denied Merrill's question either.

"Lifting now," Strike said.

The sisters chattered as the shuttle flew north. It was the kind of 'I've missed you' talk which humans used when they'd been apart for a long time. The mountains were an hour's flight north from Fia's house. We reached them just after 2 a.m. local time. I was yawning by then. It had been far too many hours since I'd slept properly.

"Okay. You're meeting Adar and Kutub here. They're both ex-Starnavy Commanders, and they're part of my network of contacts here," Strike said. "You can trust them. They'll keep you safe."

I hope, I thought.

We left the shuttle and walked over a rough pavement of rock. Howin and the troops had turned their head torches on, and the base of the mountains came up out of the dark ahead of us. "That jagged gash in the bottom of the hill is the entrance to the cave," Howin said.

5.6 minutes later a tall broad black-skinned man wearing field clothes with light armour over them came out of the crack. "That's Kutub," she told us.

I saw Fia's hesitation, then she said, "It's cold out here. Let's get inside where it's warm."

"Follow me," Kutub replied, and walked back to the

crack.

He took us into a twisted maze of large and small passageways which sloped steadily downwards. Eventually the passage ahead of us widened. Our way was blocked by what looked like an armoured shuttle airlock door.

My anxiety spiked. The last time I'd seen a door like that it had been closing off a room in an illegal mine. We'd removed Fia from slavery in that mine.

I really hoped Strike had got this right, and that we weren't leading the sisters into danger.

CHAPTER TWENTY THREE

The door opened onto a rough rock passageway that sloped steeply downwards. There were no lights. Kutub and the troops turned on their head torches to illuminate our way.

We went downwards for 12.3 minutes. The passageway ended at another closed door. This one was armoured too, and I thought it was made specially to fit the space. Kutub pressed his thumb to the keylock, and the lights on the panel turned green. The door rumbled slowly open. My back was stiff and my head erect as I waited to see what lay beyond it. Would it be people with guns?

Stop it, Snap. These are Strike's contacts. Except that Strike wasn't infallible. He'd thought the machine intelligence Chan was an ally. Until she'd tried to kill him.

The room beyond the door had plassteel lined walls. So we'd reached the bunker at last. Armoured carrycases were stacked against the far wall. Folding tables held coms terminals or pads, and twenty people bustled around in there. They all wore light armour, but nobody was pointing a weapon at us.

The squad was still bunched up around the sisters, and I

followed them into the room. A short red-haired woman bustled towards Fia. "Glad you made it," she said. "Strike told us you were on your way."

"Adar? I didn't know you were involved with this… whatever it is," Fia said.

"Planetary defence network," Adar replied. "Why wouldn't I be? Davion is my home too. I'm ex-Starnavy. I have good expertise to share."

"Right. Yes." Fia sounded surprised by that.

"Let's find you somewhere to sleep," Adar said. "Follow me."

The back of the room had four doors leading off it. Adar led the Vatan sisters and the squad through the left-hand one. "Sleeping rooms in there," Kutub said.

We chose rooms, and I settled down to sleep beside Nyla. Now all we could do was wait and see what Jorrak had planned for Davion and its colonists.

The first of Jorrak's ships appeared in orbit around Davion 3.1 hours later. It was the frigate *Hollowfire*. Strike didn't wait for the rest of the group to appear. He challenged the ship's captain right away, and sent us a feed of the contact. "This is the Davion Defence Force. Please identify yourselves. What are your orders?" he asked.

A pale-skinned man with a lined face scowled out of the console's screen. "Commander Jabar Azurian," he barked. "My orders are none of your business."

"I ask because I received this file as I left Ataret," Strike said. "Sending it over to you now."

I wondered if the ship's machine intelligence would accept it. After the attack on Strike by Chan, he'd got much more cautious about which files he accepted now.

I knew what files he was sending. Bahar and I had worked with him to select the data for them. Those files contained evidence that Jorrak was personally ordering Starnavy ships to follow Bryssa Meir and her campaign team. They contained evidence that Jorrak's troops were arresting Bryssa's supporters for unspecified crimes, then releasing them without charge.

The files were accompanied by an analysis done by our Unit contact Quindarius. He was an independent scholar, and knew just how to pull patterns from the data. The patterns he pulled from this data showed harassment by Jorrak's troops which stopped just short of election interference.

"Study those files, then you'll understand my concern when a large Starnavy force turns up over a wildworld for no good reason. I need you to check that your orders are legitimate."

"You accusing me of being a traitor?" Azurian snarled.

"No. I'm worried that you might have inadvertently got caught up in our President's shady dealings. I'm sure you wouldn't want to be associated with those."

To our relief, the Commander did accept the files. We watched him scroll through them. He was quiet for an uncomfortably long time. Then he looked up and said, "So Quindarius compiled this data? I know of him. Dandy, but a fine mind. And famously impartial. So he believes there is partisan use of the Starnavy by our current President."

"He says the data indicates that." Strike wasn't going to say yes.

"We received our orders to come here from the local Commander at Ataret Station." Azurian looked down. "I've just called up the files. They have no Starnavy headers or identifying codes."

"So," Strike said. "You have a decision to make. Do

you carry out these potentially suspect orders and kill
innocent people on a peaceful planet? Or do you question
their legitimacy?"

CHAPTER TWENTY FOUR

My heart thudded as I watched the feed. Kutub paced around the cave behind us, too wound-up to sit. We'd got many of Davion's people to safety, but some would die if this went wrong.

After 8.7 minutes Commander Azurian spoke again. "I've tried to get confirmation of my orders from Starnavy HQ. Nobody there knows anything about them. From which I deduce that they're false. I'm receiving an advisory from *Starflash*. Someone has started dropping troops on planet. I did not order anyone to land." He spaced the words out, and his voice had a snarl in it. "Do you know why they might've done that?"

"There are some people down there who know some truths our President wouldn't wish shared," Strike said. "Those people are innocent civilians."

"This feels bad to me. I'm designating *Starflash* as a rogue. I've issued orders to send our troops down. I'm proposing we work together. You don't shoot at me, and I don't shoot at you."

"Agreed," Strike said. "My troops are already on planet. And you need to know that there will be a squad of

Starnavy ships arriving here soon, under my command. They're tasked with defending the planet."

"The troops under my command are dropping now," Azurian replied. "We need to agree a command structure."

"I've been liaising with the colony's security people for several months now, advising them on defence matters," Strike said. "I'd like my troops to take advantage of the network of contacts I've built here. So I'm proposing that my people focus on defence on planet. I'll defer to your command for anything spaceside."

He gave a crisp nod. "Agreed. If you already have good planetary links, it makes sense to use them. I might need to call on your squad's muscle spaceside if we get into a fight up here."

"Agreed," Strike said. "For your information, the two ships which have just downjumped are *Arrowfire* and *Nightlance*, and they're part of my squad. I'll update you as the others appear."

"Link to Captain Sannat, my coms officer, on the codes coming over to you," the Commander said.

"Acknowledged. Will do."

Over the next few hours *Starblood*, *Blackthunder*, *Lightningflash*, and *Starflame* joined Strike's squad. Then ten Unit ships had joined us, then twenty, then thirty. By the time dawn broke over Fia's house Strike's defence squad was in place. So far, Azurian hadn't asked how we'd managed to organise such a large squad. I hoped he stayed uninterested.

The ships still loyal to Azurian sent down their troops as fast as they could. Twenty ships had defected to the rogues, and he needed the Unit's support now to even the numbers. Strike and Azurian rearranged their forces, spreading their ships out over three-quarters of the planet. Jorrak's squad had bunched up over the vast Kylen Ocean, and we wanted to keep them there.

Strike suspected Jorrak hadn't expected any opposition here. He'd expected his thugs to take over Azurian's squad, and probably kill the Commander if he resisted the takeover. Instead, we now had a very large number of Starnavy warships on our side, and an 'uneasy standoff', as Strike called it, was in place.

We all knew the Starnavy had access to weapons which could blast a planet apart. Strike was relying on the ships' captains refusing to fire those weapons. He'd told us that they used those extreme situations when selecting captains. Those who were too 'trigger-happy', as he called it, didn't get commissioned.

At least, that had been the case until Jorrak started assembling his squad.

I couldn't afford to frighten myself that way, so I made myself useful and accompanied our troops to check out the cave complex we were in. There were two ways into this bunker from the southern side of the mountains, where we'd arrived from. There were three entrances on the northern side, but they were longer routes. The bunker was protected by shields as well as doors, but we couldn't count on them keeping Starnavy troops out.

Strike kept updating us on the number of troops Azurian had designated as rogue. The count now stood at over three hundred, outnumbering the forces Strike and Azurian had sent down. If that large number mounted a serious assault on the bunker's entrances they wouldn't hold. Strike was reassessing his plan to hide the sisters in here.

"Hostiles approaching from the south," Strike warned. "Three big armoured skimmers. Hacking their coms now."

Don't ask how Strike was able to get into supposedly secure systems. I was just glad he could. It had saved our lives several times.

"Right," he said. "This is not good. Troop complement of those three skimmers is a hundred. All armoured. They've got orders to search the caves for 'traitors to the Collective'."

"Otherwise known as people who oppose Jorrak," Kutub replied.

"Indeed. They've been shown images of the Vatan sisters and ordered to make 'eliminating them' a priority. This changes things. You can't stay there."

"We couldn't withstand an assault by those numbers anyway."

"No." Now the worry in Strike's voice showed. "We never planned for this. We'd expected a few rogues we could fight off. You're going to have to evacuate."

"I agree with that analysis," Kutub said. He took it calmly. This was a Starnavy person used to working in danger – and with machine intelligences.

"They're definitely going for the southern entrances, so you need to go out the northern side. I'll arrange for shuttles to pick you all up as soon as you come out. Make sure the Vatan sisters stay safe. I've got drones outside now, and I'll give you a warning when the hostiles approach. You need to leave now."

The scene erupted into a whirl of hurrying humans. I walked over to the far end of the cave, out of their way. I couldn't help them pack their gear. There was a sense of urgency to them, but they worked efficiently. Within 6.7 minutes all their gear had been locked into its carrycases and those cases were loaded onto gravsleds.

"Alert." Strike's voice came from one of the few pads that were still active. "Hostile skimmers have reached the southern entrance. "Troops disembarking. Fifty… Seventy… still counting. Carrying assault weapons." Was that an edge of panic I heard in Strike's voice? I thought so.

Kutub took charge, detailing people to handle the gravsleds. Howin led us and the sleepy Vatan sisters out of the cave ahead of the equipment convoy. Adar was guiding us. "Set up your feed on this channel," she said, and gave us the frequency.

This cave is a twenty minute walk to the outside, she

said, switching to the feed. *Most of it's uphill.*

She led us on at a brisk pace, her head torch illuminating the passageway ahead of us. It was wide, and had flat places between those strange growths that all caves had. Bahar had told me they were formed by water carrying minerals in it and re-forming them into those columns. I couldn't imagine how small drips of water could build such big solid structures.

Some of my ancestor cousins had lived in caves. I wouldn't like that. I was a lion of open spaces. Well, I was when I wasn't on Thunderstrike, but I wasn't your typical lion.

We walked in silence for 12.2 minutes, then Strike contacted us via our feed. *Hostiles have just entered the cave*, he told us.

The passage ahead of us curved to the right and climbed up again. Adar went on ahead, and after 4.5 seconds her footsteps stopped. She swore.

Problem? Howin asked.

Yeah. A big one. Rockfall. The way ahead's blocked.

CHAPTER TWENTY FIVE

We'll have to backtrack, Adar said over our feed. *Next exit is back a ways.*

Move it, Howin said, and the troops behind us turned around and hustled the sisters off down the passageway.

We'd passed a junction 5.2 minutes ago, but this time we reached it in 2.4 minutes. *Go right,* Adar said. *And watch out for stalactites.*

This passage was rougher, and my paws slipped on some sections. It dipped down and curved around to the left. That worried me. We were supposed to be going up, not down again.

The rock beneath my paws grew wet. *Slippery ahead,* Adar warned. *Watch your footing.*

The sound I was picking up was more of a roar than the gentle murmur of a stream. As we walked towards it the noise became louder.

What is that? Howin asked.

It should be a stream, Adar said. Her voice betrayed worry. *We've had a lot of rain this last week. I think it's found its way into here.*

The passage curved to the right, and as I cleared the

curve I saw a wall of water thundering down from high on our right. It rushed across our path and disappeared into a dark hole to our left.

This is new, Adar said. *Those fissures weren't here a week ago.*

Do we cross that, or go back? Bahar asked.

Cross it, Strike said in our feed. *Hostiles are into the caves now. You don't have time to turn back.*

Don't fret it, Strike, Howin said. She moved to join Adar at the head of our party. *We'll shoot a line over that and clip on.*

She unclipped the dart gun from her shoulder and fitted a dart with a line attached, then fired it off across the stream. The dart thudded into the far wall, breaking off chips of rock as it went in. Howin tugged on the line, putting her full weight on it.

"Secure," she said. She fired a clamp into the wall behind her and secured the other end of the line. "Let's go."

Rance went over first, clipping his armour's line to the guide. *Very slippery*, he said over our feed. *Go slow.* He stumbled twice wading through the knee-high water. Then he was over, and Howin was getting the sisters harnessed up. They had waterproof field gear on, so I hoped they wouldn't get too wet in the crossing.

One by one they crossed the river, then Howin was clipping me to the line. Even with four paws, the crossing wasn't easy. The push of the water was strong and hard to resist. It reached half-way up my flanks. I had to raise my head to stop water splashing into my nostrils. When I got to the other side Rance unclipped me, and I walked a little way from the others and shook the cold water out of my fur.

When everybody had crossed over Howin released the line. Rance led us into the passage, which finally started to climb. We were going the right way at last.

Everyone went quiet, concentrating on picking their way over the rough rock. After a while I realised the splits in it formed steps. Had someone cut these to make the passageway easier to climb? It didn't work for me.

The steps levelled-out, and the roaring of the river was far behind us now. We walked on for another 20.1 minutes, then Adar said, *Halt. Quiet.*

We all stopped. My sensitive ears caught the sound of feint footsteps in the distance. *I can hear people walking.*

Over to our left, I said.

Adar swore. *That's the parallel passage down. There's an open connection to this passageway around the next curve. They could see us there.*

What's your recommendation? Howin asked.

Which way are they going, Snap? Can you tell? Bahar asked.

Downwards.

Then we'll stay here until they pass, Howin said. *We'll need all lights out. Shut down the gravsleds,* she ordered.

I've sent my drones into the northern entrances, Strike said. *I should've sent them before.*

What're they showing? Howin cut off Strike's fretting.

Coming up on the hostiles now. Oh, big squad. Thirty of them going down.

We're well outnumbered, Howin replied. *Definitely stay still and quiet. We can't fight our way out of this one. Just hope they pass the access by and don't investigate.*

CHAPTER TWENTY SIX

We huddled in the dark for 15.7 minutes while the hostiles passed us. They made a great deal of noise, and I suppose that was intentional. Were they trying to scare us on their way in'?

My heart was thudding, and I tried not to fidget. The sisters sat in a huddle on the rough rock. Their bodies were tense, but I could see them taking deep breaths, trying not to panic. The troops stood motionless. Were they trained to do that?

The footsteps were very loud, and I could hear the rustle of clothing and the clink of metal as the hostiles moved. I tried not to fidget too. They were passing very close to us. We'd be in real trouble if they came in here. Surely they'd notice this cave opening and investigate?

In the other passageway, a new conversation started up. It puzzled me. I recognized Kutub's and Adar's voices in it. What was going on? The voices were going away from us, down towards the bunker.

Got drones ahead of the hostiles now, Strike told us. *I'm leading them downwards with this fake conversation. Wait five minutes, then go.*

The hostiles' footsteps grew feinter. My ears told me they were below us, and I thought they'd picked up their pace.

Go, Strike said in our feed.

Adar moved off, leading us up at a fast pace.

You have 10.6 minutes before they reach the bunker and realise they've been tricked, Strike said.

It'll be close, Adar replied.

Sending a drone your way now, Strike said.

I saw it flicker up by the cave roof 3.2 minutes later. *Got visual of you. You're 5.7 minutes from the entrance at current speed,* Strike advised.

Let's try to reduce that, Adar said. *The rock's smoother here.*

The humans started jogging. I started to trot, but the steps were set at awkward distances for my stride, and I had to trot-jump to take some of them.

As I went up I could feel cooler air on my face. We were getting close to the entrance.

You're 2 minutes away from outside, Strike said. *And, the hostiles have just reached the bunker and realised nobody's home.*

The cold air increased, stinging my face, and suddenly the echo of our footsteps around the passageway died.

You're outside, Strike said. *Shuttle's directly ahead of you.*

Howin took off across the rock, herding the sisters towards the shuttle. It was stealthed, and only the ramp and airlock showed up, illuminated by one low light. We followed them.

The airlock door opened as the sisters reached the shuttle. *Alert*, Strike said. *Hostiles have sent a shuttle your way. Run.*

Howin hustled the sisters up the ramp of the Xenophon. I was behind them, and trotted up the ramp with the rest of the troops on my heels.

Strap in, Strike said as we tumbled into the passenger compartment. *I'm launching right away. You're the diversion. Everybody else is finding cover now.*

The shuttle lifted and turned around as I plonked myself down on the deck. The motion made me feel sick, and I closed my eyes and swallowed hard. We were climbing fast.

"Hostile's following you," Strike announced. "Shields

163

are up and weapons hot. It's another Xenophon."

So the shuttles were evenly-matched. Apart from the enhancements to our drive which Strike had got done. Somehow the thought didn't reassure me.

Hostile's weapons are live, Strike said. *Seal up.*

The troops, Bahar and I sealed our helmets. The sisters weren't wearing armour, and the troops helped them get into EVA suits while Strike started throwing the shuttle around. Howin cursed him several times before the sisters were suited. At least now they were sealed up I couldn't smell their sweat – or their fear. It helped me to keep my own fear under control.

"Oh. We've got a second pursuer," Strike announced. "Coming up from the other side of the planet."

I wanted to say that wasn't fair, then I remembered a conservation I'd had with Bahar about that a while ago.

'The Universe isn't fair, Snap,' she'd said. 'The Universe doesn't give a damn about puny humans and their petty, stupid squabbles.'

She'd been angry about a pointless conflict we'd got tangled up in, but now I saw a darker meaning to her words. She meant that the Universe didn't care whether we survived or not.

"I've called Azurian and asked for reinforcements," Strike said. "Now we find out how good our agreement with him is."

CHAPTER TWENTY SEVEN

We waited in tense silence for 10.7 minutes until Strike said, "Reinforcements have arrived. They'll escort you back to my shipbody. Sending you coms from Azurian now."

"Shuttle *Huwa*. On whose orders are you engaging *Thunderstrike's* shuttle?" That was Azurian's coms officer.

There was no response to the challenge. My heart was thudding as I waited for them to respond.

"Hostile's disengaging," Strike said. "Turning around. Heading back to *Fireblood*." We could hear the relief in his voice.

"We going to get a Phase Two?" Howin asked.

"Can't tell yet. Getting you aboard my shipbody now."

Strike went quiet while he docked us in his vehicle bay. As the shuttle touched down he said, "*Fireblood's* breaking orbit. Rest of the hostile squad are following. Guess they got scared off by Azurian's challenge."

I was still tense, expecting an attack, but it didn't come. Strike let us out of the shuttle into the vehicle bay. We went to the rec room, and everybody unsealed their suits.

"Sending you new coms from Azurian now," Strike said

as we all flopped into seats. "*Fireblood*, confirm your orders for Davion." The Commander's voice came from the nodes.

Strike put up the nav plot on the rec room wallscreen. "Not answering. They're running for jump," he said.

We watched the dots move. Ten, twenty, then the rest of the hostile force moved away from the planet and finally disappeared into jump. "That's the whole bunch," Strike said.

"*Thunderstrike*, I've just received new orders to follow that group of ships," Azurian said.

"My orders are to remain here," Strike replied. "Thanks for your help."

"I'd appreciate you filing a report on the situation here."

"Will do," Strike confirmed. "Safe journey."

He cut the line, and Bahar said, "What now?"

"I check in with our contacts down on Davion to make sure there are no more nasty surprises down there. If not, it's time to return Fia and her sisters to the planet. Fia, you'll be pleased to know that your house is intact. I think we stopped the hostiles before they could do anything really dangerous."

"That's good," Fia said. "I'll be glad to get home."

"I need to know how Bryssa's campaign is going," Merrill said.

"We can accommodate that," Strike replied.

"We'll come down with you," Bahar said, and looked at me.

"Yes, we will," I confirmed.   Bahar knew that I needed to see Nyla was settled and safe on Davion.

Strike's reports came in from his Unit contacts over the next few hours. While he waited for them all the humans caught some sleep.

I was exhausted too, and went to my quarters to sleep in my familiar and comfortable cat bed. When I woke I felt rested, and hungry. Strike fed me a yivant haunch, and I gobbled it up. He said Bahar and the sisters were awake too. Most of the troops were still asleep.

I came out of my quarters as the sisters and Bahar were leaving the galley. We went to the rec area to talk.

"We're only a week away from election day now," Strike said. "My sources tell me Jorrak's done some very questionable things in the last month. Which may or may not include ordering his thugs to murder a prominent netjockey."

"Wow!" Bahar said. "I didn't expect that, even from him."

"Yes. If he thought that would shut down criticism of him, he guessed wrong. Fellow netjockeys are determined to 'uncover the truth of his death' as they put it. And they are raking up some muck."

"All of which is a long-winded way of telling us to lie low and shut up," Merrill replied.

"Actually, no. Now the 'jockeys are on the case, I think you'll be a little safer. You'll still have to be careful, but I think my contacts on Davion can make it safe for you to continue campaigning."

"That's great," Merrill said. "I'm itching to get back to it."

Fia looked at Nyla. "Will you join us, sister? There's room for you all at my house."

"Can we all vote from there?" Merrill asked.

"I'll check local registration regs," Strike replied.

We boarded the shuttle four hours later. By then Strike

had registered Bahar and the sisters to vote on Davion. He'd also asked some of our Unit contacts down there to make sure Merrill and Nyla had secure coms to the groups they were working with.

We settled ourselves in the passenger compartment and Strike took us out of the vehicle bay. It was late afternoon over Fia's hemisphere when we landed at her house. Everything looked like it had the first time I came here; the house with its veranda, the smallholding with its neat rows of vegetables.

Strike let us out of the shuttle, and Fia led the way to the front door. I remembered she'd left it unlocked when we departed in the middle of the night. She pushed it open and went inside. Everything seemed to be the same there too.

We'd been very lucky to avoid Jorrak's troops. I hoped we stayed safe until election day.

Merrill and Nyla spent that last week before election day talking to people over the com, and doing endless data searches and analyses for Sister Strategy and False Manifesto. The sisters constantly watched election newscasts, and cheered every time data they'd uncovered about Jorrak's bad dealings showed up in them. Which seemed to be every time they watched now.

I attracted attention from the six small cats who sort of lived at Fia's house. They were all my wild cousins, but they seemed to have adopted Fia. They took some time sniffing and prowling around the other sisters before accepting them.

I played with them around the smallholding, games of hunt-and-chase. They were fierce little hunters, and caught their dinners easily each day. I felt frustration when I watched them. I couldn't talk to them, or understand what they were thinking. They had no language. Their lives were simple. Eat, play, hunt, sleep. They had no knowledge of human Presidents or elections. Their world was the present moment. I sometimes wondered if that would be a better way to live.

On the evening before election day I sat on Fia's porch with Bahar to watch the sun go down, and I told her how I felt about the cats.

"I know many things," I said. "I am so different from my wild cousins. They don't understand how important tomorrow is for humans. I feel lonely because of that sometimes."

Bahar kneeled down on the deck and put her arms around my neck. She laid her smooth cheek against my furred one. "I'm so sorry, Snap. They isolated you by giving you that knowledge. Made you into a new species. I promise we'll go find the other Predatorbots when this is over."

"If there are any more still alive," I replied.

Everyone was up before the dawn on election day. The humans were travelling into Davion's capital Paldin to vote. They ate a huge breakfast, then there was a last-minute flurry of checking they all had their IDs before we got into the shuttle.

Strike lifted it, and took us to the main shuttleport. It was already busy. Bahar and the sisters found a café which opened early close to the central polling station. The place was almost full already.

The humans drunk coffee until the polling station opened it doors. The sisters went to vote first. Bahar stayed with me at the café. Whey they returned, looking satisfied, Bahar went to vote. Strike told us he'd already voted.

I found it strange that humans' whole system of democracy depended on them tapping one box on an app on a screen. Bahar said it was what the mark represented that mattered. People who were free to choose their leaders had votes – and the power to vote people out of office. That's what today was about, getting rid of Jorrak. We hoped.

We stayed in the city until dark, then Strike took us back to Fia's house. The sisters stayed up late into the night, watching the election results coming in.

Bahar and I left them to it. As we settled down to sleep she said, "The results will take days to be collated. No point in staying up late."

On a fine morning four days later the election result was declared. We all gathered in Fia's living space as she turned on the wallscreen to watch the official announcement.

We needn't have worried about the result. Sister Strategy and False Manifesto had done their work so well that Jorrak's share of the vote was very low. Bryssa had won by a huge margin. A 'landslide victory', as Strike called it. And the person with the second-largest number of votes was female too. For some reason, the sisters cheered at that too.

"We did it!" Merrill said. "We finally got rid of the monster."

"We did." Fia went out to the kitchen, and returned with two bottles of a red liquid. She set them on the table and went to get glasses. "I know it's early for drinking," she said as she poured out the deep red stuff. "But we have something very important to celebrate. This is redberry wine, made by my neighbour, and I've been saving it for this."

She handed the glasses around to the humans, then held hers up. They did that clinking-their-glasses-together thing which Strike said was called a toast. I thought toast was something they made from bread.

Fia held her glass up high and said, "To a new beginning."

CHAPTER TWENTY EIGHT

A month later Thunderstrike downjumped at Central Station. "Very busy here," Strike said as he acquired the nav plot. "We were lucky to get a berth."

"The Unit fixed it again?" Bahar asked.

"It did. Jamar got us in here."

He didn't put his shields up, but I could sense his tension as we made our slow way in to station. We had to change course several times, and it took us five shipboard days to reach our berth. Strike was in constant contact with Unit members all the way in.

We were on our way to Bryssa Meir's Investiture. Jorrak had tried to contest her election, but a re-count had confirmed her landslide victory. We'd finally got rid of Jorrak.

We were carrying Merrill and Nyla with us, and while we made our way into dock the sisters contacted their friends in False Manifesto and Sister Strategy. Nyla also talked to the contacts who'd been part of Bryssa's campaign team.

They'd managed to get us seats in the VIP area for Bryssa's Investiture. Strike had to explain to me what that meant. Humans need ceremonies for everything. Strike said this one was more important than most. This was the way Bryssa would show the whole Collective that she was now in charge.

Nobody knew where Jorrak had gone. He'd slunk away 'with his tail between his legs', as Bahar put it. Strike said there was a lot of nervousness about whether he'd disrupt the Investiture.

I went down to Earth with Bahar and the sisters the evening before the Investiture. We took the Xenophon down to Yuwotan. Strike said that was Earth's capital city. It was in the centre of a large landmass which Strike said used to be called China.

As we came down to the shuttleport on the edge of the city its buildings spread out below us. I'd never seen such a huge area of a planet built over. Strike said that's why humans left Earth originally. They'd polluted both the land and the oceans so badly that it threatened their lives. Looking down at this sprawl, I could see how.

The shuttle landed at Yuwotan North Shuttleport. "I'm being told to clear the pad fast," Strike said. "Skimmers should be outside when you disembark."

Bahar stood up. "We're going," she said, and led us to the airlock.

The skimmers were there as promised, and they took us to the Zan Pavilion Hotel. *Very expensive,* Strike told us over the feed. *It's close to Union Square, so you're right on site for the Investiture. And you have ground floor rooms.*

Thank you, I replied. I knew he'd done that for me.

Just don't tell the Starnavy it's paying for them, Bahar said.

It's not. I paid for them out of my publication fund.

Oh, right. Bahar sounded surprised.

I was too. Strike had been writing a guide to why democracy was important, and why everyone needed to take part in electing our leaders. It seemed that he'd quietly published it without telling any of us.

It was going dark as we drove along the capital's roads. Strike had paid for parking spaces at the hotel too, of course, and we left the skimmers in the yard at the back of it. He said Earth was 'ridiculously expensive', and we'd be leaving this 'money sink' immediately after the Investiture.

The humans ate dinner in a restaurant two doors down

from the hotel. I went with them for company. When they'd finished we walked back to our rooms in the dark. I worried about us being attacked all the way back. I told myself that Jorrak's Starnavy rogues were no longer operating. He wasn't going to cause us any trouble in future. Was he?

We got back to the hotel safely, of course, and everybody went to sleep. It would be a big day tomorrow, and we all wanted to be properly rested to enjoy it.

We took our places in the stands two hours before the Investiture began. Bahar said there was a 'carnival atmosphere' to the gathering, whatever that meant.

Strike had volunteered his drones and our troops to help local Security today. The Security Chief was so pleased to have the extra help that he didn't think to question Strike's orders.

At the start of the event music played from nodes all around the square. "Makes a change from Jorrak's military marches," Bahar said. "This is… softer somehow, and more expansive."

I didn't know what she meant by that. Predatorbots

weren't taught about music at all. Why would we be? We couldn't kill anyone with it.

This is not the day to be cynical, Snap, I told myself. This is the day to celebrate.

Snap, may I access your processors? Strike asked over our feed.

I was puzzled. *Why do you want to do that?*

You experience the universe through my architecture. I want to do the reverse today. I want to experience this gathering through your senses.

I don't know how to do that.

Just let me have access.

I gave him access, and immediately my body felt like I'd been taken over by something huge. No, that wasn't quite right. It felt as if I was sitting close to my friend, our bodies touching, as we both watched the same images roll before us.

It's warm there, Strike said. He meant the temperature he was feeling from my face.

It is. We were sat in a roofed row of seats, but it was still very warm for me. That was pathetic. I'm a lion. I was made for hot grasslands.

Except, of course, that I'd never lived there. I wasn't sure if any of my wild cousins still existed in what used to be called Africa now. Maybe I should go looking for them sometime.

Are you sad, Snap? Strike was picking up on my mood.

Not exactly. I don't know what I feel. Oh, they're starting the ceremony. I felt oddly relieved when Strike's attention switched to the scene on the stage.

A woman in a black suit walked out to the table-thing they'd set up there, carrying a heavy book. She placed it on the table and opened it to a page with great ceremony. I told you humans have lots of rituals. This was one of the grandest I'd ever seen.

The crowd in the square below us was vast. Tiers of seats lined three sides of the square, closing the crowd in. The stage took up the whole of the fourth side. People were crammed into the space so tightly that they could hold each other up if they feinted.

That's the Promissory Book, Strike said. *Took 'em Standards to find the right name for it.*

Why? I asked.

Because before then leaders had always sworn to be

good while touching religious books. Most of those religions later turned out to be problematic, and now most humans don't practice them. So they had to find a new text which included everyone. They wrote a new one. Strike knew the answer to my question, of course.

The crowd in the square exploded into cheers and applause as a lone woman wearing a scarlet trouser suit stepped onto the stage. It took me a moment to realise that it was Bryssa.

Bold choice of outfit, Bahar said.

Lots of meanings to the colour red, Strike replied.

We watched Bryssa approach the table-thing with its book. She walked slowly, with her head up. She almost looked like she was relaxed in front of that vast crowd. Her thick blonde hair had been braided and the braids were coiled tightly around her head. She wore a heavy gold chain with a pendant on it which looked like some kind of logo.

She reached the table, and the cheering died. *Such power to command so vast an audience,* Strike observed. I wasn't sure whether he admired that, or whether it worried him.

Bryssa began to speak. The words she used were grand and measured. She talked about everyone being free, and every Collective citizen being equal. She talked of righting injustices.

Standard politician-speak, Strike said. *But somehow, this time I believe her.*

I could sense his emotions through our link, and they encouraged me. After all the darkness and corruption we'd dealt with in the last few Standards, I'd expected Strike to be more cynical about this change of President. But he wasn't. There was a joyfulness to him, a sense of hope for the future.

We watched Bryssa take the oath, as Strike called it. She finished speaking, and raised a hand to wave to the crowds. *Well, that's it*, Strike said. *She's officially sworn in, and Jorrak didn't attack her. I reckon that's a good day's work. It was far more satisfying watching that than I expected.*

Life will be different for us in future, I said.

The Special Investigations Unit had been formed to uncover Jorrak's bad actions. We'd done that, and I didn't know what the Unit would do now. Did it have a future?

What was our future?

CHAPTER TWENTY NINE

Strike withdrew from my processors, and the weariness which always hit me after I'd been in his architecture threatened me now. I pushed back against it, forcing my weary body to walk beside Bahar out of the square and back to the hotel.

We piled into the skimmers and set off for the shuttleport immediately. We made it to the Xenophon just in time for Strike's departure slot, and he hurled us into a darkening sky. As we left atmosphere I laid my head on my front feet and finally allowed myself to sleep.

We returned to a busy Central Station, and Strike had to stand off from station for an hour before he got permission to dock the shuttle. In the past, that kind of delay would've had him fretting about being attacked, but today he didn't seem worried.

Bahar didn't either, so I allowed myself to relax too. We got aboard *Thunderstrike* without any problems, and everyone went to the rec room.

The humans were part-way through their third cup of coffee when Strike said, "We may have a problem."

"What now?" Bahar's scent immediately spiked to anxious.

"You and I have been summoned to a private meeting with our President on station a.s.a.p.," he said. I could hear the fear in his voice. "I think she might've discovered the Unit."

CHAPTER THIRTY

I went to the rec area to watch Bahar's meeting with the President. Strike had sent a drone along officially this time, so he could stream the conversation to me.

My body was shivering as I settled down to watch the vid Strike put up on the wallscreen. Was this the end of the Unit? Was this the end of me? I shook my pelt vigorously to try and get rid of the shivers, but they wouldn't go. For once, Strike didn't tell me to relax in his snarky voice. That told me he was really, really, afraid.

I roused myself to to watch the vid as Bahar entered the President's office. She gave Bryssa a crisp salute.

"Sit down, Captain." The President's voice was neutral. We couldn't read anything of her mood in it. "I've been passed some files on *Thunderstrike*. My informant suspects that Strike has been operating without Starnavy orders on several occasions. I need to get your response to that allegation."

"I'd ask you to consider the source of the information, Ma'am," Bahar replied. "We know ex-President Jorrak recruited parts of the Starnavy for his personal purposes. Are you sure this isn't part of that squad's rumourmongering?"

"Why would he single you out for that?"

"Because we crossed paths with ex-President Jorrak's forces on Reeva," Strike said. "I received a request for help from the planet's Chief of Security. The Governor there had been bought by Jorrak, bribed to allow a mine to extract rare minerals. We rescued colonists who'd been snatched from their homes and taken to work there as slaves. I made that wrongdoing public. If these allegations came from Jorrak, then I suspect his motive is revenge against me.

"I was attacked by the *Nebulafire* at Reeva. My investigations revealed that the ship was part of Jorrak's personal Starnavy force. I have extensive files on who had been recruited to those forces, which I will send you if you wish." Strike was trying to deflect attention from us.

It didn't work. "Send me those files," Bryssa replied. "But that doesn't deal with all my concerns. Some analysts suspect Strike of having turned rogue."

Bahar said nothing. I could see her struggling to stop the shivers. This was what we'd always feared, and now that time had come. The Unit had been discovered.

"No, I have not turned rogue," Strike said. "But I did form my own unit to report on the dealings of the rogue named Jorrak. My Special Investigations Unit was responsible for uncovering most of the data on his illegal and suspect dealings." Strike's voice had a waver to it, and I think he wanted to keep talking to calm himself.

"The Unit has thousands of members, both human and machine intelligence. None of them are traitors. They are loyally doing their jobs on stations and planets. The Unit's remit is to ensure the Collective's officials operate within the terms of the laws which give them their authority. The Unit has a Charter which governs how its members operate. I'm sending that over to you now."

The waver was gone from Strike's voice. Now I heard the fierceness which signalled his belief in what he was doing.

The document appeared on Bryssa's console, and she sat down to read it. Bahar took the opportunity to unclench her hands and take a few deep breaths. I couldn't manage that. My body was wound up tight and my right hind leg was twitching.

Right now, our continued existence balanced on the

sharpest knife-edge you've ever known. Where did I get that saying from? It's ridiculous. Breathe, Snap. Panicking isn't going to help you any more than it is Bahar. I took a deep breath, then another, and the panic receded.

"Now Jorrak is gone the Unit's purpose is largely achieved." Strike said. "And I cannot hide and skulk any more. If I am deemed a traitor and uninstalled, well, I always knew that death was the danger." His words were a defiant challenge.

"Uninstall you? That would be murder," Bryssa said sharply. "No. No-one's going to do that. None of the files I've seen show any evidence of you trying to overthrow the President or the Administration. I'm not sure a charge of treason against you would stick anyway." Her words surprised me. A tiny sliver of hope rose in my heart.

"The Unit has no intention of overthrowing anyone," Strike said. "We just want to see elected officials operate honestly and fairly."

Bryssa smiled. It startled me, and I could see it had startled Bahar too. "I do intend to operate within the law," she said. "That will make things very difficult at times, but it is what I signed up to. So, Strike. I have a proposition for you. I need an accountability buddy, and you're the perfect person. It's going to take some time to root out all of Jorrak's corruption. You're the perfect person to help me with that too. Your extensive networks save me from having to build my own."

"Are you saying you're making the Unit legal?" Strike's voice was carefully neutral.

"I am. I want you to keep operating under the radar as you've been doing, but report to me direct."

"And do you promise to take action on those reports?"

"You're bold to make that challenge, Strike. Luckily for you, I appreciate that boldness. Yes. I promise to take action on all wrongdoing which the Unit reports to me. So, do we have a deal?"

"We sure do." The relief in Strike's voice was clear.

"Good. I have your first assignment. I want you to shut down all offshoots of the Predatorbot Programme which you can find. He should never have done that."

"With pleasure, Ma'am," Strike said. "But I've got to ask what you intend to do with any Predatorbots I find."

"We will have to give some thought to the dogs. But as I understand it, the enhancements done to the cats were extensive enough for them to qualify as full Collective citizens. I intend to pass an Executive Order decreeing that. It's within my powers, and as our previous President created them, it seems satisfyingly appropriate."

"It does indeed," Strike replied.

I flopped down on the deck as the vid from the President's office cut off. Relief made me weak, and I laid my head on my front feet and closed my eyes. I was going to be a legal citizen. I was no longer under threat.

"Well, Snap, that went better than I could ever have dreamed," Strike said. "No more hiding for both of us in future."

www.ingramcontent.com/pod-product-compliance
Lightning Source LLC
Chambersburg PA
CBHW020656120726
47906CB00001B/298